Erotique

The Wapshott Journal of Erotica

Issue 6

The Wapshott Press

Erotique, The Wapshott Journal of Erotica, ISSN 1947-5349, ISBN 978-1-942007-03-6 is published at intervals by the Wapshott Press LLC, PO Box 31513, Los Angeles, California, 90031-0513, telephone 323-201-7147. All correspondence can be sent to The Wapshott Press LLC, PO Box 31513, LA CA 90031-0513. Visit our website at www.WapshottPress.com.

Erotique is always seeking quality original short stories, novelettes, and novellas. Please have a look at our submission guidelines at www.Ero.WapshottPress.com or email the editor at editor@wapshottpress.com

Cover: "Untitled (nude), watercolor, charcoal, 2010," by Carol Colin, www.OrangesSardines.com

Erotique

The Wapshott Journal of Erotica

Founded in 2009

Issue 6, Autumn 2015

Edited by Ginger Mayerson

Collected Stories
David W. Landrum

Table of Contents

Goosey Goosey Gander

Goosey goosey gander,
Whither shall I wander?
Upstairs and downstairs
And in my lady's chamber.
There I met an old man
Who wouldn't say his prayers,
I took him by his left leg
And threw him down the stairs.
---Mother Goose

Everyone in town knew the White Goose Inn was a house of prostitution. Cressida, the madam, employed two younger women, Amelia and Allison. One would wait bar while Cressida and whichever of her employees happened to be free serviced men. The priest of the town, Father Claus, repeatedly tried to close the place down, but the men of the village availed themselves of Cressida's services and covered for her so he could not prove her business was a den of iniquity. He racked his brain trying to think of a way to expose her sinful enterprise.

At last, he realized only one stratagem would serve to uncover her practices. Sinful, he admitted to himself, but it would be for the good of the community and he could confess and be absolved after the constable had sent her packing—her and the two young whores who worked for her.

As a soldier, before he took his priestly vows, he had learned the importance of good reconnaissance. He went to a local pub and met with a couple of men who had frequented the White Goose Inn but had since abandoned their sinful behavior and regularly attended his church. He asked them about her establishment.

"Why will no one name her as a whore?" he asked over mugs of ale one summer night.

"She has protection," Wye, a grizzled old tanner, answered.

"Does she hire thugs who protect her and make sure her customers pay and do not expose her sinful trade?" Claus had done some reading on brothels and learned that this was how the women who ran such dens of iniquity regulated their customers.

"No," Wye replied after swallowing a huge gulp of ale. "She uses a different means."

Blount, the second informant, learned toward Claus. "She uses sorcery."

Claus could not hide his smile. If he could convict her of sorcery, she would be burned, not merely run out of town.

"Men who don't pay her or who go blabbing about what she does end up the losers," Blunt continued. He raised his eyebrows. Claus did not understand. "They lose," he clarified, "what men value the most—though no one knows how it is done."

"Ah. Like what happened to Peter Abelard."

Everyone in town knew the sad fate of Peter Abelard, a priest who ended up emasculated for getting a woman pregnant.

"Not exactly," Wye put in. "Those who see the bodies say it was not a clean, even cut such as Father Abelard received. It was a shredding, as if it were clawed away by a demon."

Claus set out the next morning, arriving early, hoping to be the first man through the door. At the entrance he saw a fresh, fair wench sweeping the steps. She smiled merrily at him. Behind her stood a large, white goose—a gander.

"Good morning, Father," the girl said.

"Good morning to you, daughter." The goose stepped closer to them. Claus admired the bird, especially its snowy feathers. He reached out to stroke the creature's neck.

"I wouldn't do that, Father," the girl warned. "He is not a friendly bird. He'll take your finger off before you know what happened. Would you be seeking Mistress Cressida?"

He nodded.

"I imagine you wish to pray with her?"

He caught the sly look in her eyes and the subtle intonation she gave to the word "pray."

"Indeed I do."

"She has devotions this time of day," the

lass returned. "I'll see if she can share some of her sacred hour with you."

She went in. Claus heard her ascend a set of creaking stairs. He looked down at the huge goose. Its beauty tempted him to stroke it, but he remembered the wench's warning. He did not want to lose a finger.

The girl returned. "The mistress would be pleased to pray with you, sir. Go up the stairs and through the door to your left."

Father Claus hurried up the stairs. He trembled, his member hard, his mind nervous over the upcoming experience. Opening the door, he saw her lying in bed, red hair spilling over her shoulders, breasts and loins as brilliantly white as the feathers of the goose he had seen downstairs.

He feasted his eyes on her body—the first time he had seen a woman in her naked glory. She smiled at him, her heavy breasts with big red nipples rising slowly as she breathed. Below them he saw her flat, soft stomach and, below that, a wild tangle of black hair through which he could see her opening. His blood jumped, and he felt he might lose his seed into his breeches (he managed to calm himself). She had long legs covered with a sheath a light hair.

"I don't have all day," she said, opening her arms just slightly in a gesture of invitation.

He clambered up on to the bed. This would be his first time ever.

Even as a soldier he had been pious. When his troops captured enemy territory and did their will upon the women there, he would go his tent and pray. When wagons brought in a load of raucous, laughing whores for the troops, he found some task to do that would keep him occupied while they were there. It seemed an irony that he was giving up his long-preserved virginity to a common drudge, but the sacrifice would be worth it. He would rid the town of a moral criminal, a bandit who robbed men not only of money but of their integrity and virtue. It was a sacrifice he had to make. As he climbed into the sheets, she lay back, spreading her legs and tilting her cunt upward so he could enter her.

He took her in his arms and pushed. The sweet, enveloping warmth went through him like the stab of a *flagellare*, the whip he used for self-mortification—except, of course, it sent flashes of joyful ecstasy and pleasure rather than sharp flashes of pain. She rolled her bottom and pulled him close so he felt her breasts against his chest and the heat of her breath on his face as she kissed him. She thrust her tongue into his mouth and hooked her legs around his ankles.

He thought, from what other soldiers had told him, his experience would end quickly. "You don't last that long the first time," more than one friend had told him on the rare occasions he had discussed the topic. For some reason, though, he kept thrusting into her but the anticipated climax did not immediately seize him. She held him, her arms strong, and moved her body against his as she moaned, squealed, and sang. He felt himself going mad with delight and with desire. She seemed determined to draw pleasure from him as one draws juice from a ripe fruit. He seemed to tumble and plummet in bliss and delight as she moved and writhed beneath him.

Then it seized him. He shouted and roared as he emptied his seed into her. Spasm after spasm shook his body. After loss of all his sensibilities in a madness of pleasure, he lay still.

She swatted him twice on the rump. Somehow he understood that she wanted him to climb off her. He withdrew from her. The tenderness he felt made him gasp and exclaim as he did. He rolled to one side. He did the same so they were lying facing each other.

It was not over, he saw. She bit his ear and his cheek, kissed him and called him her champion, her stallion, her lover made of iron and stone. He lay in the warm sheets of her bed, tongue-tied, gaping at her amazing beauty. She smiled at him, her eyes big with delight, her body streaked from the motion of his body against her.

"You're a marvelous man," she said, "and a sweet lover. You can pay me three gold crowns for my services."

A smile of a different sort spread over his face.

"A sweet lover I am, and the last lover you will ever have, strumpet," he said, his triumphant smile widening. "I plan to tell the city of your sin—how you seduced me, how you run a house of prostitution, and, I am told, how you practice sorcery. You will burn for this last item, though the others are serious sins as well. I will confess my lapse and be restored to a state of grace. Your girls—well, I don't know what will happen to them, but your future is not rosy."

"Yours isn't either," she replied. "Though, like a rose, it will be very red."

He heard shuffling and turned. The goose, white as an angel's wings, stood a foot away. He felt vulnerable in his nakedness and started to back off. He heard the woman's voice behind him.

"Goosey gander!" she called loudly.

The goose spreads its wings, lifted its head, and hissed at him.

Two days later the local Bishop announced that Father Claus had died in "an unfortunate accident, the details of which are unseemly to relate." The village got no further word on it. Another cleric took his place and the matter soon receded from public memory. The morning of his demise, Amelia and Allison cleaned the trail of blood that led from Cressida's bedchamber, down the stairs, out the door, and over the front steps of the White Goose Inn. Some travelers found his body a mile down the road. That afternoon, business at the inn went on as usual.

No one saw the goose for a while. Some speculated that he had gone wild and flown off into the woods. He returned a week later, feathers discolored to a sort of ocher hue. Opinion held that he had encountered a fox in the forest, had been bloodied by it, but escaped, found a refuge, and spent a week healing until he was well enough to return home. Nature took its course, the goose preened himself, grew new feathers, and soon his magnificent plumage shone a spotless white once more.

Cressida, Amelia, and Allison quietly continued their profitable business.

A Discourse with the Incorporeal Air

The university had never produced a stage play that featured nudity. Sossity Chandler had never acted Shakespeare. Somehow, though, the two things seemed to work together to her advantage. She saw the call for auditions and read the note done in red so no one reading the notice would overlook it: **PART OF GERTRUDE WILL REQUIRE ACTRESS TO APPEAR TOPLESS IN ONE SCENE.** That night she ran the idea past her suite mates. Nerissa, from Greece, said she thought Sossity should audition. "In Europe, girls go topless on public beaches to get a tan," she said, "And we don't even think it's a big deal." Kathy Farisi was dead-set against it and expressed shock and disgust that her friend would even considering such a thing. "It's sleazy. Besides, what would your family think?" Cheryl, her roommate, reacted more judiciously. "I probably wouldn't," she said, "but if it's done right and the nude part really contributes to the overall effect of the scene, I'd say, fine." Sossity had hoped for an opinion that took aesthetics into consideration and decided she would audition.

"You'll probably get the part just because you've got big tits," Kathy responded sourly when she learned of Sossity's decision. Sossity did not have to worry about what her boyfriend, Brian, would think about it because they had split up a month earlier.

She went to the studio the next day. Quite a few women had come to try for parts. The director was playing Horatio as a woman (renamed Horatia); Rosencrantz and Osric would also be played by women. As she got in line, she wondered how many of the women were auditioning for those parts or for Ophelia and how many would be willing to play Gertrude. When Sossity appeared before the director and her advisers, they asked her which part she wanted.

"Gertrude."

The director, a woman named Amy Cogan, asked if she had seen the statement.

"I saw it."

"You're willing to play the scene topless?"

"I don't have a problem with that."

"Have you ever played a part on stage that required nudity?"

"No. But I've been nude in the locker room a lot; and with more than one boyfriend, if you would call that public."

Amy laughed. "I was thinking on stage, but I like your attitude. What have you acted in?"

"I played Emily Webb in *Our Town* and was Maria in *The Sound of Music*—both of those were in high school. I was Nellie Forbush; we did *South Pacific* in a local production just before I came to school here." She paused and added, "I wasn't topless in any of those roles."

"Especially not as Maria, I suspect. You've never acted Shakespeare?"

"No."

"Well, let's have you read one of Gertrude's speeches."

She read through one, trying to show a little of her dramatic abilities. The panel listened carefully. Sossity thought she had done well and left the theater feeling good about the audition. She, Kathy, and Cheryl went to the gym and worked out. Sossity swam a mile at the pool after her suite mates went back to the dorm. When she got there, a message waited on her email. She had got the part. "Five women auditioned, Amy's message said, "but you nailed the dialogue. Rehearsals began at the end of the week."

On Wednesday she had a date with Jerry Watanabie, a guy she had been out with twice. He owned a plane and had offered to take her on a flight. They rose above the campus at dusk. She took in the beauty of the sky and the lengthening shadows below them. After landing, they went to Quincy's Bar she told him about the role she had landed in the upcoming Shakespeare play and that through part of it she would be topless.

"Do I get a preview?" he joked. The remark caught her off guard. After a moment nonplussed, she laughed at his audacity. She also resolved, because he had pleased her so much with what he said, that she would give him a glimpse of what the audience would eventually see.

"It doesn't bother you that I'm doing that?"

"I grew up in an émigré community. There were enough of us that we maintained a public bath in our town. I've been looking at topless women—my mother and sisters included—since I was a kid." Jerry was Japanese-American. Sossity decided, after hearing that, that tonight was the night to sleep with him.

At her place that night, she melted in his arms, stretching, feeling him thrust into her, shouting when the surge of orgasmic joy captured her. After the spasm passed, she held him tight, squeezing her strong thighs together (she ran varsity track for the university) and shaking her bottom until he came. Afterward, he ran his fingers around her nipples. She quivered.

"I'm grateful for the preview," he said. "You're beautiful."

If he had made some silly remark about having to share the sight of her tits with a big group of people, she would have written him off as a twit. But she liked his humor and subtlety. She liked it, too, that he appreciated her breasts. He lavished praise on them, kissed, licked, and caressed them—so much she had a small "after-orgasm" from his touching her. They went back to the airport, flew to Indianapolis, drank more, and came back home. She did not settle down in her room on the bed opposite Cheryl's until 3 a.m.

In the morning, she told her suite mates she had the part. Her announcement caused a stir in her suite. Nerissa and Cheryl sided against Kathy, who for some reason reacted bitterly to Sossity's announcement that she got the part. She wouldn't go with the others to breakfast at the dining hall. Sossity got her alone in the room after Nerissa and Cheryl had left for classes.

"What the hell is wrong with you?" she demanded.

"Why are you letting them exploit you like that?" Kathy returned.

This puzzled Sossity. Kathy was conservative and not an ardent feminist. Words like "exploit" did not come into her vocabulary a lot. Nor was she moralistic. She went through boyfriends at a fairly rapid pace and ended up with sleeping with most of them.

"It was my choice. I wanted the part. I plan a powerful interpretation of my character. As for exploitation—the director is a woman, for Christ's sake."

Kathy didn't reply. She was grumpy for the next couple of days.

Sossity went for the read-through and then to the first rehearsal. "You don't have to play the scene topless until we perform it," she said.

"People need to get used to it," Sossity said. "And so do I."

~~~

She put all her heart into acting the next few rehearsals. In the scene that had so riled Kathy, Sossity, as Gertrude, Hamlet's mother, is getting ready for bed when her son comes in to confront her. Mother and son argue. When she tries to leave, he seizes and, as Amy framed the scene, tears away the loose top of her garment. She covers herself at first, holding a flap of torn cloth in front of her, but after Hamlet kills the spying Polonius, Gertrude apparently forgets to cover up and plays the remainder of the scene with her breasts bare. Only when Hamlet confronts her about having sex with the king does she cover herself. After Hamlet exits and Claudius enters, Gertrude lets the cloth fall away. After hearing her speech, he wraps her in his coat.

Amy's staging made the scene powerful and memorable. The actors who played Hamlet and Claudius, however, kept forgetting their lines. At a director's critique session, Amy told Sossity, "Those marvelous boobs of yours are distracting the guys. We may have you play it clothed."

Sossity did not want this. She had specifically chosen the part so she could be nude on stage, a thing she had always wanted. And there was Kathy. If Amy changed the staging, Kathy would think she had "won."

"I'll see what I can to make them more comfortable," Sossity told Amy. "I really want to play the scene the way we first envisioned it."

At the next rehearsal, Marcus, the actor playing Hamlet, did a little better. The cast took a break for lunch. Sossity did not bother to put a top on. She sat down at a table stage left, breasts bare, and sipped a cup of coffee. Marcus slid into the seat across from her, noticed her lack of dress, and started to get up.

"Sorry," he said.

"About what? Join me for a cup of coffee."

He gaped a moment and then said. "Sure." He got a cup of coffee and returned, sitting across from her. Still, he was nervous. He had flubbed a couple of lines today. His eyes kept wandering down. She smiled.

"Like what you see?

He grinned and nodded.

"I like being bare," she said. "I especially like it after rehearsing in that heavy, layered Renaissance costume. It makes me sweat. This is better. Cooler."

"Sure is," he answered. "Very cool."

"You made a Freudian slip," she laughed. "Do you go with the Freudian interpretation of the play?" she asked. "Like in the Olivier version? Mom and son are sweet on each other? Oedipus complex and all that?"

"Not too much, though it would be nice if the characters in the play were sweet on each other."

"It sure could be. Come here." She got up and walked into the folds of a stage curtain. After a bewildered moment, he followed her into the concealment of thick cloth.

Once inside, she kissed him. His hands

immediately went to her breasts. He squeezed and caressed. Sossity reached down and rubbed his crotch. He was in costume, wearing tights and a codpiece. She felt him respond to her touch.

"I like the codpiece," she said.

Marcus laughed. Actually, it's a dance belt, like ballet dancers wear — but the next best thing."

They slipped into a nearby room and closed the door. Marcus sealed it shut by leaning a board against it. The room, used for storing theater props, crowded and dusty, did not allow them to lie down. They stripped. Sossity squatted.

"We can't do missionary position in here. We'll do it native style."

Marcus, erect and ready, knelt in front of her. Sossity twisted herself into position and lowered down, grunting and sighing with pleasure as she enfolded him. She put her arms around him and clasped her legs around her backside. After a moment, she began to move, slowly going up and down, hearing the squish and slop of her wet pussy as she bobbed, waves of delight coursing through her. She had not thought she would come. Marcus kissed her and stroked her hard, swollen nipples, almost putting her over the top. She resisted the rising tide of joy building in her, not wanting to come too soon. She moaned, tried to be quiet but did not succeed very well. A deep-bought orgasm exploded from her coccyx to the top of her head. She moaned, flailed, and jerked and then clung limply to

Marcus. After less than a minute, he followed, his cries as loud as hers had been.

They held each other. Sossity reveled in the heat, the juice, their hearts pounding almost audibly, the closeness and intimacy of the moment; and, for Sossity, the thrill of marvelous sex with someone she hardly knew.

"Did you wear a condom?" she asked groggily.

"Sure I did. Didn't you see me put it on?"

"I had my eyes closed."

They got dressed. Marcus peeked out the door. The coast was clear. They slipped outside and returned to table where they had been drinking coffee. Two other cast members came by and jokingly told Sossity she ought to button up her blouse. They seemed not to have noticed the post-orgasmic red streaks on the whiteness of her breasts.

Rehearsals went a little better, but Amy still talked about editing the topless scene out of the play. At coffee with Marcus and Phil, she asked about Amy.

"Is she married?"

"Divorced," Phil said. "It wasn't that long ago."

"What do you think of her?"

"She's beautiful. She used to act. I did some TV. Her divorce really beat her out of shape."

"Maybe she needs to get back into shape. I

want to save that scene. If we take it out, the power goes out of the production."

Amy reacted with surprise the next day when Sossity invited her to a party.

"Well, it might be nice," she said.

"I've invited some other cast members. It will be a good mix of people."

She hoped Amy would not come up with any nonsense about the director not fraternizing with the actors and she did not. Sossity invited Ruth Wong, who had the feminized role of Horatio and Lainey Griswold (Ophelia); besides Marcus and Phil, two other male cast members Matt (Fortinbras) and Jamal (Polonius) promised to attend.

She thought the mix would work well.

The party was held at Jerry's place. His family had money, he was an only son, and his mother and father paid for his housing (*and about anything else he wanted*, she smiled to herself). The large apartment had a well-stocked liquor cabinet and Jerry said everything in the house was theirs to use. Sossity bought beer and snacks. It rained that night. Her guests arrived, accepted drinks, and started talking and laughing.

When Amy and the others were mellow from liquor and talk, Sossity suggested they all do their favorite Shakespeare scenes in whatever degree of nudity they chose. She started the show, doing her scene as Gertrude. Her guests watched with appreciation. When she finished, anxiety pulled at her insides. What if no one took up her offer? Lainey/Ophelia came to her aid. She did the scene where Hamlet terrorizes Ophelia. She bared her small, pale, beautiful breasts in the bright light of Jerry's living room. She played the scene in a way that suggested Hamlet had broken in one her just after she had got out of the shower. Everyone laughed and cheered.

Marcus got up next. He stripped to his shorts and did Claudius' prayer, after which he mooned the audience. The partiers had shaken their inhibitions by now. Ruth stripped and had everyone in stitches by doing her character's speech describing the ghost's appearance but doing it as if she were fully dressed and nothing unusual—such as being stark naked—could be connected with her recital. Sossity had run track with her, had seen her in the shower many times, and admired her big tits and the small, neat tuft of jet black hair above her opening. Ruth had a beautiful body. The men there were admiring her. When she finished her monologue, she did not get dressed but sat down and started drinking beer and talking with Matt/Fortinbras.

After Ruth stepped down, Amy walked up on stage.

She stood a moment and then stepped out of the minidress she had worn. She shed her bra and, after a little hesitation, her panties. She had a strong tone body, a generous swath of hair between her legs (Ruth had once told Sossity, who was of British and Dutch origins, "You northern European types have the advantage," she said. Giving her friend's public tuft a tiny pull she added, "I wish I had a sugar-bush like that!") Amy began Juliet's soliloquy, the famous, "Romeo, Romeo. Wherefore art thou Romeo?" people laughed and applauded at her suggestive rendering of the lines about a name: "it is nor hand, nor foot, / Nor arm, nor face, nor any other part / Belonging to a man." When she came to the end of the scene where Juliet, not knowing Romeo is listening, invites him, "Take all myself," Amy was started and reacted when Marcus came on stage as bare as she, saying the right next lines: "I take thee at thy word: / Call me but love, and I'll be new baptized; / Henceforth I never will be Romeo." Both of them laughed and continued the scene.

"'What man art thou that thus bescreen'd in night / So stumblest on my counsel?'" Amy intoned in her role as Juliet.

Marcus answered as Romeo: "'By a name / I know not how to tell thee who I am: / My name, dear saint, is hateful to myself, / Because it is an enemy to thee; / Had I it written, I would tear the word."

"'My ears have not yet drunk a hundred words / Of that tongue's utterance, yet I know the sound: / Art thou not Romeo and a Montague?'"

They finished the scene and kissed.

After that, Amy reached down and began to stroke him. They continued to play the scene. She knelt, kissed and licked his member until he was stiff. She stood and said, "Let's go do the wedding night scene." The two of them made their way to a bedroom.

Sossity glanced over at Ruth and Matt. They kissed. Matt squeezed her right breast with his left hand. His right hand was in her pussy. He slowly and expertly pleasured her. Sossity saw the look of rapture on her face. She glanced about for Lainey but did not see her—or Jamal. She felt arms around her. Jeff had come up behind her. He put his hands over her breasts.

"'Lady, shall I lie in your lap?'" he asked, quoting *Hamlet*.

"'No, my lord,'" she answered, taking up the game.

"'I mean, my head upon your lap?'"

"'Ay, my lord.'"

"'Do you think I meant country matters?'" He emphasized the indecent double entendre Shakespeare had put in this land, saying *cunt*-ry.

"'I think nothing, my lord.'"

"'That's a fair thought to lie between maids' legs.'"

"I hope you mean what you say," she laughed, breaking off the recitation.

Ruth had come by this time. After her shouting, moaning orgasm, she got to her knees and was giving Matt a blow job. Her long black hair spread over her shoulders, her head moved up and down in steady, easy rhythm, slurping, sucking, gagging sounds escaping from her throat. Sossity led Phil into the room where Jerry kept his computers. A large, comfortable couch lodged in the room. She and Jerry had screwed on it several times. She lay on her stomach. Phil took her from behind as she draped over an armrest. As he fucked her in a slow, deep rhythm, she gasped with pleasure but also smiled knowing Amy was in the next room enjoying a passionate roll with Marcus. The play would have the topless scene. Sossity concentrated and worked her way to an orgasm that brought a small scream to her throat. Here she could make all the noise she wanted. This time, she thought, to celebrate her success. Knowing Phil's prowess as a lover, she thought she might go for a second one.

Ruth and Matt went home together. Lainey and Jamal woke Sossity up at 2 a.m. (she had been sleeping soundly after two orgasms back to back) and told her they were leaving. Phil had an early class. After a quick screw, he left for ECON 231. Sossity feel back asleep and woke at eight. She banged around in the kitchen and soon heard someone stirring in the main bedroom. Amy was up. After a while the shower came on. Looking fresh and happy, eventually Amy emerged from the bedroom.

"Marcus still asleep?" Sossity asked.

"He left last night. Had a paper to finish. I think you are Phil were in the computer room. Great party. Thanks for the invitation."

"I'm glad you could make it."

"I made it all right. You aren't dating Marcus are you?"

"No. He's just a fuck-buddy."

She laughed. "I'll see if he can be that for me."

"I think you guys will get along well. Have you decided whether or not to leave my topless scene in?"

Amy laughed again. "After tonight, how we could even think of cutting it? I'm tempted to put a little more skin in now, but I don't think the school would go for that. I had a hard enough time getting permission to do your scene. I wish we could get one in for Ruth. Isn't she beautiful?"

"She sure is. I envy her."

They ate breakfast and talked about the production. The scene was secure now. As they were finishing, Jerry returned. Sossity introduced him to Amy. The three of them talked over a coffee as the clouds cleared and the sun broke through for the first time in several days.

A Big Cat

Marci and I just finished a post-coital joint when we heard a familiar thumping noise downstairs. It was Ribbs, our cat, pulling on a window screen.

"You let her in," Marci said. "I'm too stoned to walk."

I was not much better but I got up, threw on a pair of track shorts and a t-shirt, and went downstairs.

I opened the door and went cold when I saw a police cruiser pull into my driveway. Two cops got out. The cat slipped in as they came up the front steps.

They were big guys, as most cops are. I stared at them, dumb.

"Mr. Daryl Shepherd?"

I nodded, realizing that anyone who even took a glance could tell I was high.

"I'm Officer Thompson, this is Officer Collie, of the Grand Rapids Police Department. May we come in and ask you a couple of questions?"

Still unable to speak, I stepped away from the door, stumbling as I did. I reeked of marijuana. They came in. I stood by the piano and faced them.

"Mr. Shepherd, we wonder if you know Jason Vanderkodde."

The name registered slowly in my mind.

"Yeah, I know him."

My voice sounded slurred and thick. This was not good.

"Were you aware, Mr. Shepherd, that Jason Vanderkodde deals drugs?"

I tried to act surprised but could also tell they saw through my act. A knowing glint shone in their eyes. Before I could answer their question, Collie let out a tremendous sneeze then four more short but forceful ones in rapid succession.

"No, I didn't know that."

Collie sneezed twice more. These were not little sneezes. Thompson looked over at him.

"You okay, Hal?"

"I'm fine," he answered, his jaw tight.

It occurred to me that Collie must be allergic to cats. I also realized he probably had not admitted this to anyone because such an admission would have disqualified him from being a cop. I bent down and picked up Ribbs. I moved close to the two police officers, making sure Ribbs was on the side nearest to Collie.

"Jason Vanderkodde was arrested for possession of marijuana this afternoon," Thompson said. "We found your name and phone number on a list he kept on this person and we wondered"

Collie went into a sneezing fit. He sneezed repeatedly, unable to stop. He began to wheeze as well.

"Sorry, Gerald. I've got to get out of here."

He stumbled toward the door, barely able to walk due to another sneezing fit. I stroked Ribbs, who purred and watched Collie with curiosity.

Thompson hemmed and hawed. I answered his questions as vaguely as I could. Whatever information he got from me would be useless without another officer to validate it. He had probably planned to question me and, if he had sufficient reason to assume I had bought drugs from Jason, search the house. But he could not do this with his partner gone. He kept asking questions and waiting for Collie to return. After ten minutes and no Collie, he instructed me to pass any information I might get about Vanderkodde's drug dealing to the Grand Rapids Police Department. I told him I would. He left.

I put the cat down. She sauntered into the kitchen and flopped down in a favorite spot by the refrigerator, near where we kept our stash of dope.

I went upstairs to the bedroom. Marcie lay on her stomach.

"Did you let the cat in?" she asked.

"Sure I did. You know what they say: a big cat is dangerous but a little pussy never hurt anyone." I stroked the tuft of hair between her legs.

"You're such a damned dumb-ass," she said, laughing and sighing with pleasure as I continued to stroke her. "I thought I heard voices down there. Were you talking to someone?"

I lay down and put my arms around her. I kissed her.

"Just the cat," I said.

Encounter

They parked a hundred yards from the shelter they had found. The sun hung above the horizon of Lake Michigan. Purple and burgundy clouds towered upward. The beach, clear but for a few driftwood logs, darkened, its scrub grass casting shadows and the waves falling in a sure, slow cadence.

As they kissed, she remembered how much she had missed the lake. The man she had been married to for so long would never bring her here. Once or twice she had come on her own or with the children, but never with him. And though she kissed her new lover passionately, the kissing was not spontaneous but prescribed for what they planned to do. He opened her blouse and ran his hands over her breasts. She rubbed his jeans at the crotch. Eventually he slipped his hands under her skirt and touched her—she had not worn underwear.

Not much time passed before she said she was ready. They got out of the car. He draped a blanket over his shoulder and carried a small gym bag in one hand. They walked to a rise of stone and negotiated a narrow passage until they were inside a natural enclosure, open but canopied with trees and vines. The rock walls rose up above a floor of sand. The woman took off her blouse and skirt and lay face down on the blanket.

"Lots of lube," she said. "Remember what we read on the internet."

"Got it," he replied.

He disrobed, squeezed a generous dollop of a recommended lubricant jelly on one hand, pulled the cheeks of her buttocks apart, and spread the gel around her opening. He got more and spread it on top of what was already there, gently opening her anus with his fingers, making sure a good amount of the lubricant coated her sphincter, which would be sensitive. It was the first time either of them had done this. He did not want to cause her any pain.

"Good?" he asked.

"Um huh."

"You ready?"

"I'm ready."

He slipped on a condom and slathered lubricant on it, just like the internet sites said to do. He knelt above her.

"Here goes," he said.

She made an affirmative sound. He lowered himself and pulled her buns apart. Finding the place, hoping it would go well, he pushed into her.

He had slid in easily but heard her gasp and felt her tense.

"Carrie?"

"It's okay."

"You sure?"

"Yes. Put it in a little further. I'll tell you when to stop."

He thrust carefully another inch into her.

"Okay, stop," she said, her voice even.

A moment of silence passed. Both of them were relieved that they had negotiated the beginning so successfully, but now neither seemed to know what do.

"Well, come on," Carrie said after a moment. "Fuck me."

They both laughed muted little laughs. The man—his name was Jesse—began to move, gently, remembering what the articles they had read said about being easy, smooth, and not penetrating more than three inches. As he thrust, he heard her gasps and murmurings—of pleasure, he realized. He had felt her body relax. With that, he was able to relax as well.

Carrie rejoiced that it had gone okay. They had done it. It had hurt just a little when he put in in—the books said it would and she had had expected it—but they had got past the painful part. Warmth radiated from her perineum upwards. She enjoyed feeling his body against her back and his breath on her neck and ear. When he reached under and took hold of her breasts, waves of pleasure surged through her. She breathed out with delight.

No one would see them here, she thought.

She had insisted on doing it here despite his objections.

"Can you even think of what it will be if we get caught?" he had asked.

"We won't get caught," she said. Knowing how much sway she held over him, she maintained her desire to do it outside and he finally assented.

She slowly sank into the rhythm and pleasure of what they were doing. The fear of something that seemed vaguely sinful and slightly dangerous faded. Despite their yearlong physical relationship that had included everything but this, and despite all the research they had done, she had accumulated a lot of anxiety about it. Her anxiety fell away as she surrendered to the odd pleasure working in her body. Her mind again wandered backward.

She remembered the time she had hurt her ankle. Her husband would not buy her the crutches the doctor said she must have. Despite her frantic, amazed protests, he steadfastly refused. For a week she had to crawl—literally—around the house until one of her grown children found out what was going on and, after an angry altercation with her husband, helped her learn to use the crutches he had brought. Carrie filed for divorce a week later.

The warmth in her hips increased. Jesse moved evenly and with restraint. A rush of love for him overspread her. She felt her nipples harden and felt herself luxuriate.

"Can you reach down and rub me?" she whispered.

She did not know if he could, but he slipped one hand under to her torso. His fingers found her other opening.

Now she knew it would happen soon. She thought of the first time with Jesse. He taught English. She had begun to take classes there after her divorce. In the early days, the two of them met at conferences so his wife (whom he had since divorced) and her own children would not suspect. Her oldest daughter, though, was sly and street-smart.

"Going to another conference, Mom?" she asked her voice full of amused irony, eyebrows raised. Again, she smiled as he moved and as the pleasure continued to spread. She waited a moment, wondering if for some reason it would not happen. Then she felt it start as a tiny spot of pleasure and build until a deep, strong spasm shook her. She almost shouted as currents of joy coursed through her like the waves out on the lake.

Her orgasm set him off. He ejaculated suddenly and violently. He lost control for just a second and hurt her a little with his flailing, but the pain passed and the *jouissance* returned. Her soul sank into deep contentedness and satisfaction.

They lay quiet. She heard the waves and the gulls and saw how the light had faded and the tree-hidden cleft where they had made love was almost dark.

"We ought to go," she finally said. "Make sure you grab the condom so it doesn't come off." Then, after a moment's pause, she added, "I don't think that would be much fun."

He laughed—a quiet laugh but warm and rich. She felt a flush of love. A tiny spasm—an aftershock of pleasure—shook her, though he did not notice. He pulled out of her. She felt a bit of pain, but by this time the condition he was in made it minor. She rolled over and sat up.

He smiled, took her breasts in his hands, and kissed her as he squeezed. Another small orgasm shook her.

"I can't stop coming," she laughed. They kissed—hard kisses. She knew she loved him now. She knew she could trust him.

"Let's get dressed. No need to push our luck," she said.

They wiped off with the damp clothes they had brought then dressed and squeezed out of the rocky shelter. He carried the blanket, she the bag full of accoutrements.

A thin slice of sun posed above the horizon. The clouds had turned a deep purple and Prussian blue. She remembered how her ex-husband had tried to cheat her out of the shares in the two service stations they owned. Her lawyer had caught the ruse and stopped it. She would have all the money she needed to finish school from her part of the profits. The sun slid down, the waves churned more furiously. She felt she could stand there with him forever. Venus appeared. A wisp of moon malingered in one corner of the sky. After watching until it was dark, they walked back to her car.

The Slave Girl and the Angel Israfel

The man who purchased her went over every inch of her body. He cupped his hands over her breasts, measuring them and her small red nipples with his thumb and fingers. He felt her smooth, curved hips, probed the nest of hair between her legs, felt her shoulders and ankles, looked at her teeth. After admiring her trim stomach and the curve of her lower abdomen to the rise of her delicate mound, he nodded, gave the slave owner a bag of money, and took her out into the arches of the hallway. A eunuch gave her a cotton smock to wear. Two servant girls and a strong, handsome young man, apparently a guard, joined them as they stepped out of the slave house and on to the crowded, noisy streets of Baghdad.

Her new master looked to be near sixty and showed his age. He did not move with energy and she shuddered at the certainty she would be in his embrace, and probably not before long. She glanced at the guard. He wore a blue shirt and trousers, a white turban, and gold shoes. A round shield covered his back and he wore two scimitars in sheaths over his chest and stomach. He walked with powerful steps. She noticed the muscles of his arms and his stern, vigilant, well-formed face. She also noticed a small silver cross around his neck. Two guards, one a fair-skinned Frank, one a black Nubian, walked behind them.

The street was thronged with jostling figures hurriedly pursuing tasks, carrying things they had bought in the market, hurrying forth on errands—nothing at all like the quiet town by the sea where she had spent her childhood. Hala, from a Christian family in Anatolia, had been sold as a slave to pay a debt when she was only four years old. As a girl, she worked in the kitchen of her master's home and helped with cleaning. Her owners were kind, practiced her religion, and did not abuse her. The household she lived in was a household of merchants in a seaport town on the coast of Lebanon. Evenly divided between Christians and Muslims, people got along and the local ruler was benevolent to all religions. The family she served made a great deal of money exchanging goods with English and Italian merchants and treated her more like a daughter than a slave.

Well, she thought, as she walked along the teeming streets of the huge city, *maybe not exactly like a daughter*. At age sixteen the midwife examined her and her mistress spoke vaguely of the "new duties" she would soon undertake.

Hala understood what the mistress expected her to do and felt fear, but this melted away when she found the sole recipient of her favors would be the son of her owner. Handsome and strong, he took her virginity gently. She came to cherish when he parted the curtains to enter her room. The servants would sprinkle spices on her bed. She would strip naked and wait for him. He usually came when the first stars shone over the sea and kissed her lips and breasts as the salt breeze blew through the windows. Her secrets parts quivered and luxuriated. The hot fluids of her passion ran down her thighs and her nipples became hard like rubies. He would climb onto her in the strength of his youth and fill her with joy and ecstasy. She moaned and writhed, caught in a storm of pleasure that swept over her like the sea and shook her like moving of the earth.

Life returned to its routines. The son of the family came to her once or twice a week. She craved the days when he took her. When she knew he would come for her, she could hardly do her other duties. All of this, however, ended. The son got in some kind of trouble and had to flee the country. Soon the family sold her off. She suspected they needed money to pay bribes to the local officials so they would not retaliate against the family for their son's infraction, whatever it was. She ended up in the slave market in Baghdad.

The group surrounding her and her new owner arrived at a spacious house enclosed within a wall. The young man, who reminded her of the son of her former owner, went in and emerged a few moments later. He nodded and all of them went inside.

The compound radiated in the morning light. The house, made of white marble, sat in the shade of towering palms planted all around it. Smaller quarters for servants rested against the walls. Fountains splashed into pools and flowers rioted along the interior of the walls and in boxes and urns set by the walkways and in the arched windows. Her new owner was wealthy and liked opulence, she saw.

He turned Hala over to some women servants and went into the main house. Once he was away, the other servants began to shove and hiss at her. They bathed her, splashed her with perfume, and then led her to a bedchamber.

The bed was soft. They had spiced it. She ran her eyes over the crimson and gold arabesque designed that adorned the sensual dark blue marble walls. The gold curtains in the windows stirred with an indolent afternoon breeze. Hala waited only a few moments before the beads parted and Daryosh, her master, came in. He wore a red robe, which he shed immediately. Without speaking, he climbed in bed and mounted her.

It was not as bad as she had thought it might be. He was an experienced man and was stiff—to some degree. He finished well. But the experience was like drinking tepid coffee or weak wine—especially after the sating joy she had experienced with the son of her former owners.

She thought of his strong arms and hard cock, contrasting what she had just experienced with what she had known in the past. She tiredly realized this was her fate. She could only accept what had befallen her and best the best of it.

Afterward he lay next her. He ran his fingers over her breasts then down to her opening. She smiled but did not speak.

"You are very dear to me," he said after a while, "and you please me greatly."

"Thank you, Master," she said, keeping her voice low.

"If there is anything you desire, let me know, and you will have it."

She nodded.

"And if the other women are cruel to you, tell me and they'll be sorry."

He lingered a while. Hala felt ashamed of despising his abilities. However much age had blunted his prowess, he seemed kind and generous. Eventually he left. She relaxed. Perhaps it would not be so bad. If she were careful, she could possibly carve out a comfortable niche for herself in this place.

She dozed until someone shook her roughly.

It was the woman she had seen on first coming to the house — the woman who had shoved and shouted at her.

"Get up, you lazy whore," she said.

Hala glared at her.

"Up, unbeliever — and don't look at me like

that or I'll make you pay for your insolence."

Hala got up. The woman led her to a bath chamber. Again, she pushed her along, cursing her all the way. Hala's anger flared. She turned and again glared at the woman. She swung her hand to slap Hala, who seized her fingers and sank her teeth in them.

She bit down as hard as she could. The woman began to scream.

"Murder!" she cried at the top of her voice. "Murder! This *kaffir* is trying to kill me!" She bellowed and roared as Hala clamped her teeth with all the force she could call up.

She heard scrambling and clattering. The young man she had admired earlier in the day came bursting into the room, scimitar drawn.

Hala let go of the woman. She crumpled to the floor, sucking her fingers, crying and writhing.

The young man looked down at her a second then turned his eyes on Hala. She gazed back at him and then remembered she was naked as the day she was born. She put one hand over her intimate parts and crossed her right arm over both her breasts.

He smiled, just slightly.

"Excuse me," he said, amused at her embarrassment and at the abjectness of the woman on the floor. He turned his back and called out. After a moment, a eunuch and two serving women appeared. The eunuch and one of the serving women helped the injured woman out the door. The young man followed, giving Hala a glance and tiny *salaam*. The other servant, a girl of fifteen or sixteen years, watched the others leave, turned to Hala, and bowed.

"Will you bathe now, mistress?" she asked, her voice revealing fear.

"I will. Who was that horrible woman?"

"Her name is Fatima."

"She does not deserve such a name. Fatima, the Prophet's daughter, was wise. I never want to see her again."

"Yes, mistress," the girl said. She undressed and the two of them stepped into the bathing pool. The girl, named Anna, began to wash Hala.

Hala wondered if she had gone too far but soon found her boldness rewarded. Her master, Daryosh, demoted Fatima to the status of a scullery maid. He also gave orders that all should show respect to Hala. Anyone, he said, who abused her, in word or deed, would suffer. After Fatima's demotion and Daryosh's declaration, the household feared Hala.

She began to learn about her environment. Daryosh, from a Persian family that had lived in Baghdad two generations, worked for the city government as a tax assessor. Scrupulous, honest, he refused bribes and enjoyed the favor of the city's rulers. Widowed, he lived alone with his servants, though his sons, powerful and wealthy, and his daughters, married to influential men, lived near him and visited often. Daryosh was fair and equitable to Christian and Jews — people of the Book — and employed them in his household. His trusted cook was a Jew, his bodyguard, who commanded his home watch, was also a Christian.

Daryosh's generosity to non-Muslims had earned him the ire of the other chief tax assessor, Kharki.

"Why do you tolerate these unbelievers," he said. "That guard of yours will cut your throat someday. Your cook will poison you. I'm told your new slave girl is a Zoroastrian."

Daryosh did not correct Kharki's error. He only replied, "Religion has little to do with the jobs of those three you just spoke of — especially in the case of the girl."

Anna, the girl who had bathed her in place of Fatima, also a Christian, became Hala's primary source of information on the household.

She asked about the bodyguard. Anna told him his name was Suleiman. A Syrian, he had served in the border Army of that province from age twelve. Though demonstrating loyalty and skill on the battlefield time and time again, his status a *dhimmi*, a non-Moslem, prevented him from serving in the regular army so he had found work in as a guard for a prominent Baghdad politician. When the politician died of old age, Daryosh hired him.

At night she dreamed of him. She thought of muscular arms, his strong, straight body, and his easy, confident movements. She thought of what lay hidden beneath his clothing and what pleasure it would be to feel him. When Hala asked if he took lovers, Anna blushed. Hala smiled.

"Anna, really," she said, her voice mock scolding.

"Please don't be angry, mistress, it was only a few times, and at the last winter moon I told him not again. I was afraid I would get pregnant and shame my family."

"And why would I be angry with you for being his lover?"

But the answer was obvious to both of them.

Two months after Hala came to Daryosh's household, a merchant delivered the lute she had requested. An English girl in her old town had taught her to play. When boredom struck her, she asked Daryosh to get her one. She had learned to count on his benevolence and had begun to claim the advantages her position in the household gave her. He allowed her into the grounds of the compound and everywhere except his own chambers. On Sundays, he permitted her, accompanied by Anna, to attend church. Anna said he would grant her more freedom if she continued to be obedient.

When the lute arrived, she unwrapped it. Made of pale wood, inlaid with amber, it reflected beauty and grace. Its rounded back, curved like her breasts, felt smooth and cool. As she looked it over, Suleiman came in. He smiled at her. She had not been near him for some time. Hala fancied she blushed when she saw him. He laid his hand on the rounded back of the instrument.

"I've never seen an *oud* that looks like this," he commented.

"It's not an *oud*. This is an English lute," she said. "The town I lived in was a merchant's port. Some English and Italians lived there. I became friends with an English girl and she taught me to play."

"You were friends with an English girl?"

"We became very close. I taught her to speak our language and to bathe so she did not stink as most Europeans do. We often prayed together. Her name was Elizabeth. After many years, her family returned to their homeland. To lose her was a great sorrow."

"I'm sorry your friend went away." They lingered then he said, "And I'm also sorry I intruded upon you when you got the best of Fatima."

"I didn't mind," she said, amazed and slightly frightened at her own boldness.

"Neither did I."

"I will play some songs on this lute tonight at the dinner the Master is hosting."

"I would love to hear you. Tonight, however, he will host Fakhrul Bakr Karkhi, who will not sit with unbelievers. But I'll be near and strain my ears to listen."

"I will think of you as I play."

He took leave of her.

That night she came into the dining room. Several men who looked prominent and wealthy sat with Daryosh. Servants, Anna included, scurried about delivering dishes and pouring drinks. Hala took her place on a mound of cushions across from the table and began to play.

Her performance caught the attention of the diners. The English style music, with its unique cadences, intrigued them. Once or twice their conversation ceased entirely and they listened, all expressing pleasure expect Karkhi, who glared at her with a sour expression on his face.

"She plays beautifully," one of the guests remarked.

"I would agree but that she is a *kaffir*."

"Does being an unbeliever affect how well she plays her instrument?" another quipped.

"Do not trust *kaffirs*," Karkhi warned. "I've known many of them in my years—Christians, Jews, Zoroastrians, followers of the Buddha. Don't trust any of them."

"I trust her," Daryosh said. "How could I not? She plays like the Angel Israfel."

That night, as Anna bathed her, Hala asked about the Angel Israfel.

"He is their name for Gabriel. The Qur'an says he will blow the trumpet of God on the Judgment Day, but many legends not in their scriptures are told of him as well."

"What do the legends tell of him?"

"That his heart is a lute. That he sings more sweetly than any of God's creatures. That he loves and blesses all who truly love music and is their advocate."

Hala went to bed weary. She thought of Suleiman—of his strength and how wonderful it would be to lie in his arms. Daryosh was kind but heading toward the end of life. Much of his vital strength had gone.

She drifted off to sleep. In a dream, she saw the Angel Israfel. He looked like Suleiman but was huge and had wings. Lute music radiated from his body.

She listened, enraptured by the song she heard. She felt her body throb and her breasts long for the touch of a lover. Craving rose from where her legs joined. It radiated upwards in a sweet, twisting spiral of desire. She felt herself luxuriate. Sweat drenched her as the song continued to penetrate to the core of her soul in a steady, even rhythm. Enraptured, she listened. Her longing increased, consuming her. She reached a hand toward the angel and the song that came from him.

She felt someone grasp her hand. She opened her eyes and saw Suleiman. He put his finger to his lips.

"No," she whispered, afraid. "No, Suleiman. Please. It's too dangerous. Someone will see us."

"I've secured all doors. The house is in my keeping. I alone have the key to your room. No one will ever know."

She reached and felt him. There was no more to say. Long-practiced now in the arts of love, she spread her thighs. No need for lotion. She felt wetness running down her legs. In a moment he was on all fours, positioned over her. He took her in his arms. She felt the strength of his body and then gasped as her pushed into her.

He was like carved marble, like a ramrod, like the shaft of a battering ram. Stiff and big, he filled her with pleasure. She tried not to moan loudly as he began to move, jolting her, her body shaking from head to foot as ecstasy gripped her. Muffled noises of joy escaped her lips. Her efforts to quiet herself soon failed. She moaned and gasped, clinging to him, wrapping her legs around him, jerking and rolling her hips to match his motions. The moon climbed through the starry sky as Suleiman thrust into her with a rhythm violent and gentle at the same time. She felt pleasure build in her pussy and increase until an orgasm shook her from head to foot. Pleasure and joy rolled over her, deep as thunder from rainclouds. Then another. Finally, she felt him swell and empty a warm stream of seed into her. His deep groans filled her as and she grasped him with all her strength.

Then, quiet.

Hala felt as if she were floating in a lake of pure water under bright stars. She felt as if

Suleiman had removed her from earth and its trails and taken to the edge of paradise. She wondered if, once again, she would see the angel.

Her vision lasted only a moment. Once more, she lay in his arms, her body sated, the sweat and the fluids of their passion mingled and the heat and joy of their embrace fending off the chill or early morning.

Words, they both knew, were not appropriate. They lay there, listening to each other breathing. Both of them caught the faint noises of the city beginning to stir. The mullah would call the faithful soon to prayer. Suleiman kissed her.

"I'll come again to you."

She nodded and he stole away.

Suleiman came to Hala the next few months. She feared discovery, but his position as guardian of the household advantaged him to such a degree that could bring about complete concealment of their affair. She fell in love with him. It seemed a blasphemy to think that an angel had brought him to her. We often dream of what fills our hearts, she knew, and what is in our thoughts before we fall asleep, she mused, becomes the stuff of our dreams. Anna had told her about the Angel Israfel that night and it had been in her mind when sleep claimed her. Still, she wondered.

Her abilities on the lute attracted attention. People came to hear her play. City officials and representatives of the Sultan listened to her. High-ranking officials commended Daryosh for his hospitality. Talk arose that the Sultan might promote him to the post of assessor for the province. Hala dreamed now and then of Israfel, heard his music in her dreams, and tried to remember and to play the melodies those dreams brought to her. Suleiman stole into her chamber as often as he could and their bodies united into one song, into one pulse of happiness.

Kharki visited more frequently. He quieted his criticism of Daryosh's employment of unbelievers. He listened to Hala play and asked if he could bring some of his associates to listen. Daryosh agreed. When the first stars appeared in the sky, she and Anna went to Daryosh's dining room. Anna retired to the kitchen. Hala began to play.

She went through the numbers Elizabeth had taught her then tried to play some of the tunes she had heard in her dreams. She lifted her eyes after concentrating on a particularly difficult string of notes only to see a man standing a foot or so from her. He seized her arm and clamped his hand over her mouth. Her lute toppled to the floor, its strings sounding discordantly as it broke. The man dragged her to the center of the room and shoved her into the circle they had formed around Daryosh. A moment later, another man dragged Anna and Micah, Daryosh's cook, across the room and shoved them into the perimeter they had formed.

An evil, triumphant leer appeared on Kharki's lips.

"Daryosh the Persian, my old rival, the rivers of time have called your name. You and your whore and these other two will die. The blame will fall on Suleiman your guard and his men. I have bought witnesses. No suspicion will fall on me for this."

After fighting down his amazement and disgust, Daryosh asked, "Why, Fakhrul? I always trusted you."

"You should not have trusted me. I knew if you were gullible enough to trust unbelievers, you would certainly trust those of your own faith. And you did. You played right into my hands."

Hala listened, horrified. She realized she was drawing her last few breaths. She hoped they would be merciful enough to give her a quick end.

But as she prepared herself to face the end of it, Kharki jerked, his eyes wide with pain and astonishment. She saw a spot of blood form on the front of his robe. Then his legs buckled and he collapsed to the floor.

Suleiman entered the room. He held the peculiar weapon Hala had seen the English sailors carry at her old town—a crossbow that sent out a projectile rather than an arrow.

"Don't anyone move," he said.

The Frankish and Nubian guards who helped secure their house and several other armed men filled the room, swords drawn. They disarmed Kharki's associates.

"All of you," Suleiman said. "I know Kharki hired you and you have no stake in this matter other than money. If you will testify against him, you have my word and the word of the Master of this house that no harm will come to you and in the end we will let you go in peace. Otherwise, all of you will die on the spot—except for two who will be turned over to the rulers of the city for a most unpleasant and lingering death."

The men Kharki had hired looked at each other. They held up their hands to show they accepted his terms. Suleiman ordered his guards to secure them. Then he knelt on one knee before Daryosh.

"Master, are you all right?"

He nodded, shaken by the brush with death and the treachery of a friend. Suleiman and Anna helped him to a chair. Hala knelt at his feet and took his hands.

When Daryosh had recovered and the police had removed Kharki's body; when the deed was made known to the authorities and reported throughout the city; after Daryosh's children, friends, and colleagues had gathered around him to comfort and sympathize with what had befallen him, he called his household together and brought Suleiman forward.

"How did you know to come to my aid?" he asked Suleiman.

"I stood at the door because I wanted to hear the beautiful music Hala played. When I heard an evil sound come from her lute, I knew something was wrong and rallied the guard."

Daryosh nodded, a slight smile on his lips.

"I would adopt you as my son," he said, "but the laws of religion in our kingdom forbid me from doing so. But I will reward you with gold." He paused, and then said, "I also know you have some affection for Hala. I give her to you—give her to you as a free woman."

Rejoicing rang through the assembly. All wished Hala happiness. The one woman in the household who hated her, Fatima, had been a co-conspirator with Kharki and was in prison awaiting execution.

Hala prostrated herself before Daryosh and thanked him for giving her freedom. Daryosh had known, she saw, or suspected, or perhaps deduced what was going on between her and Suleiman. He was a kind man. She felt shame at having betrayed him.

Suleiman and Hala married and lived long, prosperous lives. The governor of the city noted Suleiman's bravery and loyalty and allowed him to serve in the garrison that protected the city walls and gates. He eventually rose to become a commander.

Hala did not see the Angel Israfel in her dreams anymore or hear his music. But she never forgot. And she always considered the source of her marriage, and of her music, to be divine.

The Dryad Grove

Barry Phipps smiled, feeling an amused surge of frustration that as a lawyer he was not allowed to have any social interaction with clients. His firm had taken the case of an ecological advocacy group that wanted to save a stand of old-growth timber outside his town. Their legal representative, Sylvia Collins, was one of the most beautiful women he had ever seen, but restrictions based on legal ethics prevented him from even speaking to her in a familiar way, let alone asking her out.

Worse, he thought, that he had to sit this close to her.

Sylvia Collins had a well-shaped face and a pretty, wide mouth; she had a nice smile. Her large eyes framed by long lashes were green shot through with brown. Tall and slender, she looked like a basketball player or a runner—trim, strong, alert. Today she had on an earth-tone blouse, a green skirt, and darker green tights. Her charm had overwhelmed him. The beauty she exuded naturally had claimed his gaze.

He shuffled a stack of papers.

"I think we have a good case," he said.

"The grove is government land because it was purchased when the state bought that section of the old Grand Trunk Railroad line. Under state law, no old-growth stands of timber can be sold off—and the grove falls within that state's definition of a stand of old-growth timber."

"If that's the case, Mr. Phipps, then what is the issue?"

"At issue is that we are up against a wealthy, rapacious development company that can hire good lawyers and wants that piece of land. Michigan law also states that the government may sell off any land if 'emergency' warrants the sale. The firm asserts that the sale will fall under the emergency clause due to the dire economic conditions that prevail in our state—and the fact that their project will bring jobs and commerce to the area, which has been particularly hard-hit by the economic downturn. To a state that is billions of dollars in debt, the sale of a property for multiple millions is attractive. And, since it's more than a mile from the scenic trail to which the old railroad line was converted, they claim it will not diminish the natural beauty there."

She shifted nervously in her chair.

"Is the state persuaded?"

"The state needs money, Miss Collins. The attorney general and the governor seem taken with the idea of selling."

"When you put it that way, it doesn't sound particularly good for us."

"We do have the law on our side—the argument comes down to natural resources versus economic development. The state needs economic development, but the people still value natural beauty. We need to make the issue a public issue, get it in the papers and TV so we can garner some public support."

"I'm working on that," she said. "I have an interview with The Press this afternoon and tomorrow I'll be making a pitch to the local FOX station to do a report on it."

"That will help. We will do the legal side and your organization can do its part to build popular appeal."

"I just hope we can do it well. Our funding is limited."

He wanted to say that her charm and beauty would go a long way toward promoting the cause; he wanted to ask her to lunch. Ethical regulations prohibited him from doing either of those things.

They concluded their meeting. Sylvia Collins departed. He noticed she did not go to the parking lot but exited through the front door. She turned and started down the sidewalk. It was unlikely she had parked on the street. Probably she used public transportation or walked. The Press was four long blocks from his office.

He sat back. The case did not look as promising as he had presented it. The state needed money. The newly elected administration cozened up to business quite a lot. They had already sold off some parcels of land up north. He hoped he could argue well enough in court to save the five-acre tract the development company wanted to turn into a shopping mall called Towering Pines.

Frustration settled on him. The girl. Lovely and charming, she undoubtedly had a crowd of men in pursuit. But as long as the case continued, he would not be able to ask her out. He turned his attention to other business.

On the drive home that afternoon he saw her walking up Michigan Hill by the Blodgett Children's Hospital. He stopped at a light just as she halted on the sidewalk across from him. He rolled down the window on the Lexus.

"Sylvia!"

She looked over, recognized him, and smiled.

"Do you need a ride?"

Her lips parted in hesitation, and then her smile took over again.

"Sure."

"Hop in before the light changes."

She hurried around and slipped into the car before the light turned green.

"Where can I take you?"

"Alberta Street—close to Huff Park."

"Were you walking there?"

"It's not that far. I like to walk."

Huff Park lay probably three miles from where they were. He remembered she was an ecological activist.

"I'm staying there," she said. "Actually, I live out by Coopersville, not far from the grove."

He remembered her resume. She had graduated from the University of Michigan with a degree in Ecological Management. She also had an MA in journalism from Grand Valley State.

"Have you lived in Michigan all your life?"

"Never left the state. You?"

"Always here."

He turned on Fuller and took it all the way to Alberta, turning into a quiet neighborhood of middleclass homes with Dutch-style gambrel roofs.

All the while they had been driving along Barry had felt his attraction to her mounting. As a lawyer he knew the dire consequences that could result from even looking at a woman too much, but he could hardly keep his eyes off her legs and face. Unnerved that he might do or say something inappropriate, astounded at how out of control he felt, he breathed a silent sigh of relief when she pointed and said, "My place is over here. You can just park on the street."

He stopped the car beside a stand of tall birch trees.

Barry turned to see her face only inches from his. She leaned over and kissed him.

The touch of her lips burst a dam of passion in him. He wrapped his arms around her, kissing her with abandon. She returned his intensity, pushing her lips to his, gasping as he touched her breasts and knees.

They were in a public place—but he did not want to stop and could not stop. Whatever spell had bewitched them, both were ensorcelled by it. His hands were under her skirt. She reached down and tugged at her tights and underwear, pulling them down so he could get his fingers into her opening. Her wetness told him how much she desired what he intended to do. After she stiffened, she dropped to her knees on the passenger side of floorboard and bent down.

Barry felt more fear. If someone came upon them, saw and reported them, it would mean jail and the end of his career. But she had already started to pleasure him with her lips and tongue, head moving in a sure, even rhythm. He had no choice but to surrender to the pleasure of it. After the deep spasms of pleasure shook him, she sat up. He stared at her as she pulled her tights and underwear back in place.

"Meet me on the west side of Huff Park tomorrow at two, where the boardwalk through the wetlands meets the walking path. I need to go now. Someone is coming this way."

He glanced out to see two boys on bicycles. Sylvia opened the passenger side door and hurried away, disappearing behind the line of white birches.

Barry sat in a daze then got out of the car and hurried down the lightly worn path she had taken. He expected to see a house behind the row of birch trees but stopped when he saw no house, only an open field and the path leading down into the woods of Huff Park.

He stood, looking around, wondering if he had misunderstood her. A breeze blew from the park below, carrying the smell wetland. He stood there several minutes and then returned to his car.

He drove away, unable to believe that he had engaged in sex in a public place with a woman he hardly knew. Regard for his career, fastidiousness to avoid the appearance of impropriety, fear of scandal, had made Barry circumspect to the point of excess. Yet in the car something had driven him to batter through the walls he had constructed to contain his desires. He realized that for the first time in years he had lost control of himself.

Confusion and bewilderment disorienting him to the point he fear he would blurt out the whole story of what had happened with Sylvia Collins if anyone questioned him about it, he pulled into the parking lot of a bar he did not frequent. He feared seeing a colleague or associate.

He drank, looked, and saw Kristi Deronda walking toward him. He needed to be alone.

Barry Phipps had two women in his life at present. Betsy Lane worked for the law firm. Tall, beautiful, making her name in the community as a skillful corporate attorney, she had cast her very pretty eyes on him. The two of them had dated off and on for three years. Betsy was at the point where she expected them to go to the next level in relationship. Kristi, whom he saw approaching him, represented the other side of his taste in women. She was quirky, unconventional, and expressive.

She came up, leaned down, and kissed him.

"I didn't know you would be here. Did you come to hear us play?"

"I have to admit, I forgot you guys were on tonight. Is it your whole band?"

"All of us."

"I have to go home, but I'll come by later to hear you play."

"You look like you barely missed a pile-up on the freeway."

"Been a long day," he said, glancing at her. Kristi had light red hair that she wore parted on one side and puffed up on the other; sharp eyes and a face that showed her quick intelligence. Kristi taught special education at Lincoln Elementary school on Crayhen Road. She played guitar in a locally popular band.

"Can I get you a drink?" he asked.

"Sure. The others aren't here yet."

She ordered a stinger. Being with her comforted him.

"What's up at work?" she asked.

"The eco case—the old-grown wood Devon Developments want to cut down."

"Oh yeah—the Dryad Wood, they call it. That was on FOX."

"I see their publicity rep is doing her job."

Kristi's band showed up just then—two

men and a woman. They did blues and pop. He enjoyed listening to them. He had another drink as the group set up. Kristi turned her guitar, did some licks on the harmonica, and talked with other musicians. He decided to head back to his house. Before he left, Kristi caught him the door.

"I know you'll be back," she said, "but I wanted to say before you, why don't you come over to my place after the show? I feel like I've hardly even seen you the last couple of months. We need to catch up on things."

He said it sounded like a good idea. After he had been home only a few minutes, he got a text form Sylvia: *2tmrow Huff Park wst brdwlk mn path*. He tried to call her but got no answer.

Barry sat down on his bed. Did Sylvia Collins intend to use what happened in his car to blackmail him? What baffled him the most, however, was the question of how he had been so overwhelmed by desire. He had cast off restraint. He had forfeited self-control. It was not as if he were a new kid on the block snagged by an aggressive *Lorelei*. Sylvia's was beautiful, but not more than Kristi or Betsy — or any of the other women with whom he had been romantically involved. What had happened?

Eventually he got up, showered, changed, and headed back to the Viceroy Bar and Grill. By the time he got there, Kristi's band was playing.

He ordered a drink and sat down. Kristi, who did guitar and vocals, sang with her usual aplomb energy. Her band did mostly blues, but she served up one of their crowd-pleaser covers, the old song, "Fever." Barry drank and listened to the lyrics:

> *You give me fever when you kiss me*
> *Fever when you hold me tight*
> *Fever in the morning*
> *Fever all through the night*

She sang it in a breathy, sexy, orgasmic-groan voice. When she finished, the crowd shouted and cheered and her band went back to its usual blues repertoire. He drank and waited until they finished at eleven. Kristi came to his table.

"You guys sounded great," he said.

"Thanks. I was beginning to wonder if you liked it. You sat here looking like you've been sucking on a green persimmon for a week."

He laughed. "Sorry. I've got a lot on my mind."

A waiter came and took Kristi's order. She moved her chair closer to his and leaned in. "I'm beginning to wonder if Betsy has made some successful moves on you."

"Not lately."

"You're not hitting on that woman who represents the people fighting for the grove of trees Devon wants to bulldoze, are you?"

He flinched. He thought to say no but found himself answering, "She kind of flirted around."

"She's pretty and very charming," Kristi

returned. "I felt a little warm toward her myself."

"You met her?"

"She presented their case to a community group this morning—I got picked to represent our school. She's persuasive and... well, I don't know how to say it. She is pretty—that's for sure and seems to send out an aura of sexiness, life, energy—it overwhelms you. I sat there and thought, *Damn, I'm getting hots for a woman*. But it wasn't that, exactly. She exudes life... vitality... I don't know a way to express what she does."

"I felt the same thing."

"I've got enough competition with Ms. Betsy Lane. I don't need this gal in the mix. What's her name?"

"Sylvia Collins. She's a client. Remember, it's against lawyer ethics to socialize with client. I know you're surprised lawyers have ethics."

Kristi laughed. They got on to other subjects. She told him her band had performed a lot lately and she was thinking of quitting her teaching job and going full-time as a musician. They drank until the bar closed and drove to her condo. Kristi made love with passionate gentleness. The episode with Sylvia, the violent onrush of overwhelming emotion and desire, had knocked Barry off center. Being with Kristi returned him to stability and certainty. He kissed her as they lay together. The warmth of her body against his felt sheltering.

In the morning they made love again, had breakfast, and went their ways. He reported to work resolved that he would not rendezvous with Sylvia Collins. Whatever had come over him yesterday, he would not allow it conquer him again. He felt uneasy, fearing someone had seen their outburst in the car and reported them. He could not risk such a thing happening again. The best way to prevent it was to stay away from her.

The morning went well. He worked on the case, studying the laws, writing notes, developing his strategy of argument. The more he worked the more he felt secure in his resolution. He had lunch with two friends from his University of Michigan Law School days. When he returned to his office, he found an email saying Betsy wanted to see him.

He went to her office, nervous, wondering if someone had seen him and Sylvia, he knocked and entered.

Betsy only wanted to clarify a point on a case they had worked on together last year. She sat behind her desk, stately, beautiful, and impeccably dressed. He knew he would eventually have to resolve their relationship, which had gone up and down but onward for the past four years. They had been intimate—one summer they had all but lived together—and her father was a senior partner in the law firm. Both these factors loomed in his imagination as insurmountable obstacles.

On either side of her desk two large queen's umbrella plants loomed up from ceramic urns. He inwardly chuckled at "queen's umbrella" plants shading Betsy. *Fitting*, he thought as he regarded her in her beige business suit, sitting at her neat, perfectly organized desk, sheltered by the bright green leaves of the two massive *schefflera actinophylla*.

As he stood there, he felt something—an urge creeping over him, as if rising from the bottom of his feet. He began to think of Sylvia Collins and the tsunami of passion that had engulfed them yesterday. The resolution he had so astutely built up in his mind dissolved in seconds. He hoped Betsy would finish soon so he could keep his appointment at Huff Park. When he left his office, he could hardly keep from running to his car.

He drove down to Huff Park and took the west branch of the main walking path to where it connected with the boardwalk that led through the wetland. Sylvia had waited for him. Barefoot, she wore tan shorts a white tank top.

He wanted to speak but could not articulate a word. She took his hands.

"Come on," she said.

They walked down the boardwalk and turned on to a path. He followed her into a grassy circle surrounded by small, spindly trees. She unhooked her shorts, let them fall to the ground, and kicked them away. She pulled the tank top over her head. She had worn nothing underneath.

"Someone will see us," he managed to say, his voice barely above a whisper.

"No one will see us."

She lay down. It seemed like the line of saplings had turned into a protective wall of thick, tall ash and birch trees so dense he could not see beyond them. She reached up to him. He took her hands and sank down as she relaxed to receive him.

He must have slept. When he opened his eyes, a circle of sunflowers ringed the bower of soft, thick grass where they lay. He reached for her. They rolled on their sides.

"Get dressed," she told him. "I'll answer the questions you have."

He got his clothes on. She stood up, shaking the twigs and grass from her long hair.

"In a moment you will see me in my true form," she said.

"This is not your true form?"

"Not my truest. Before I change into what is most true of me, know that I am carrying your child."

They had used no protection.

"You're pregnant? How you can you know?"

"I know. It is different for us. Come to the grove in two days. I will be there and you will see your child. Bring your colleagues with you."

She took a few steps back, spread her arms, and stood straight. He gaped as her body elongated. The lines of her flesh smoothed out and turned white. Her arms spread, sprouting into branches with light green leaves. In only a moment, a birch tree stood in place of the woman with whom he had just made love.

He stared, doubting his sanity. Her discarded clothing lay at his feet. The tree shimmered in the breeze. He walked over and touched its trunk with his fingertips. When he did so, he felt saner than he had ever felt. Warmth from the smooth bark flowed into his fingertips. Its warmth was her warmth and her life. He put his hand flat on the gently rounded trunk. After he had held it there some minutes, he returned to his office.

When he got there, he had a text: *rmbr: in 2 days*.

Two cars pulled up by the walking trail. The partners in his law firm piled out, looking around. Cardinals and thrushes flew across the path as they walked. Chipmunks and rabbits scurried away from the intruding human presences. Tall stands daisies and black-eyed Susan decorated the borders of the trail. The old railroad bed the state had paved and transformed into a walking path wound through wetland, farms, and near the stand of old-growth trees for which his law firm had agreed to provide advocacy.

Most of his colleagues liked the idea of seeing the place. Betsy was skeptical but kept her censure to herself. The group walked a quarter mile down the paved path then took a side trail. Two hundred yards from the main path, the old-growth grove began.

Even Betsy gaped at the towering pines and oaks. It was as if they had walked back in time to a primal era when nature, not human beings, held sovereignty over the earth—and, in a sense, they had done just this.

Silence fell over them as they walked through the quiet stand of huge trees.

"I'm glad we made this visit," one of the older lawyers said.

They stopped in front of a birch tree.

"I've never seen a birch that size," Betsy commented.

Barry knew the tree. To one side of it he saw a sapling rising out of the ground—slender, delicate in its beauty, beginning its life of growth up to the sun's warm light.

"It would be a crime to cut this down," John Lane, Betsy's father commented.

They marveled for a while longer and then followed the path back to the trail. When they came to the parking lot, Sylvia was there. She wore sunglasses and had on a white blouse, a very short print skirt, and sandals. She smiled and waved.

"Well, I see my lawyers are on the job," she joked.

Her beauty and cheerfulness charmed the whole group—even Betsy. They chatted with her. Talk turned to the case. Everyone said walking through the grove eloquently illustrated the vital of importance of winning legal protection for it.

Lane said he would place all his law firm's resources into seeing the grove preserved. He added that he had some political connections in Lansing and would see what he could do to block the development. After a pleasant, animated talk, the lawyers piled back into their cars and headed for town.

When Barry got to his office, he had another text: *Good You saw yr child I will come to u again Sylvia.*

He closed up the phone. He would have to get some plants in his office, he thought — make it a green space with plants that reflected the beauty and power of nature. He did not understand how he had previously got along without them.

The Last of the Wine

I

When I saw the crowd of people waiting for me on the shore, I knew it was time to get the wine out. I was saving it for the end, and the end had come before my eyes. The people lining the shore carried spears and bows. They played instruments that made loud, droning, disagreeable music. As I tried to turn my boat around (impossible for one man against contrary wind), something hit the hull. The sound came twice more. At first, I thought they meant to kill me with arrows, but then my vessel lurched violently. I lost footing and tumbled down. They had let fly harpoons with lines attached to them and were pulling me in to shore.

I had sailed in thick, cold mist through the last two dawns, unable to see the sun or stars, and had no idea where I was. As they pulled me closer to shore, I got out a knife, thinking to cut the lines, but decided against it. What good would it do? They had me. If I cut the lines, they would shoot out other ones or just kill me with their bows.

I was somewhere in the northlands—Europa or Vineland. Oak and laurel trees grew just beyond the beach; rocky outcroppings, moss and lichen told me it my location lay somewhere in the upper reaches of the Atlantic. As they pulled me in, I calculated the size of the crowd assembled on the sandy beach at around three hundred.

A group of burley men pulled the lines. I threw my knife away so as to not antagonize my captors. The prow of my boat hit the wet, slushy sand. The men stood thick-chested, with mighty arms, dressed in kilts and coarse tunics. Most of them had red hair and beards. Their women, in long dresses, hair braided, stood taller than any women I had seen. They looked strong and muscular, though they carried no weapons. They growled and screamed, though as I got closer, the screaming and growling quieted to a low, even chant. I could not tell if was hostile—but the eerie, tone frightened me more than the angry shouting. They had pulled my boat out of the water by now. I stood on the deck, legs shaking from fear and fatigue, ready to accept whatever Fate had decreed for me. Four men grabbed me, dragged me off the deck, and hauled me over to a thickset man with a braided beard and bright blue eyes—their chieftain, I assumed.

He looked me over and spoke. I could not understand and shook my head to indicate this, all the while trying not to show the fear that was tying my insides into knots. Two more men and a woman joined him. The men were bearded like him, though one of them had dark hair. The woman wore a burgundy cloak. A pendant decorated her forehead. She was beautiful, with piercing grey eyes, blonde hair, and an intelligent gaze. The men spoke to her and to each other in their language. She said nothing but observed me and her compatriots thoughtfully as they went back and forth in their peculiar tongue. Though I could not get any of it, it seemed from the tone that the dark-haired man wanted me dead — his eyes flashed murder when he looked at me and he kept stabbing his finger at me. The man I assumed was the tribal leader seemed to contemplate, giving me evaluative gazes as he listened. He spoke only twice, both times in an even tone. The tall woman listened.

The debate went on perhaps twenty minutes. My legs grew numb. I felt hunger and fatigue and wondered if I might collapse. I grew fainter until, in the midst of a vociferous exchange between the main speaker and the other man; the woman broke in, bringing me out of the miasma of lethargy that had stolen upon me.

Her clear, even words silenced them both. She looked from one to the other. When she had their full attention, she spoke at length. I stood there, trying not to look decrepit, thinking from her tone that she might be speaking in my favor. The men listened. When she finished, both of them nodded. The chieftain, the tall woman, and the two men departed. The guards who had taken me off the boat led me away. They dragged me to a house, shoved me inside the door, and secured it.

The dwelling contained a bed with a straw mattress and a wooden crock in one corner—a chamber pot. Reeds covered the dirt floor. I relieved myself in the pot. Fear and weariness claimed me. I stumbled to the bed and instantly was in a dark, impenetrable sleep.

I woke up hungry but rested and looked around. The small house was warm—a marvelous thing after standing on the deck of a ship for a week in rain and fog. The door opened. One of the guards brought me bread and fermented drink. I made gestures to indicate my thankfulness. He said nothing, turned, and slammed the door. I tried not to eat too quickly. The warm bread tasted like food from paradise after my long diet of salted preserves. The fermented drunk had a bitter flavor, but its full-bodied tanginess refreshed me. I remembered I had left my wine on the boat. As I finished eating and drinking, the door opened again.

The tall woman, accompanied by two girls dressed identically to her, stood silent and stately at the threshold. She nodded. One of the girls walked off and returned leading young woman who was dressed in a rough, coarse garment. Her feet were bare. They pushed her inside. The door closed.

In the light shining through cracks in the shuddered windows, I gazed down at her. She was small, delicate girl, with the bright red hair so common among these people. Freckles covered her face and arms. Her limbs and feet were delicate; her eyes a soft blue, her teeth white and even. She blinked with her long lashes.

We stared at each other. Finally, she pointed to the bed. At first I did not understand, but the look on her face told her meaning. "No," I said, shaking my head. She shook her head in the affirmative. When I persisted in my refusal, she pointed (with her thumb) at the door and then ran her finger over her throat, making a sibilant noise and then gazing at me. She pointed to herself, put her hand beside her neck and jerked it upward, tilting her head. So that was it. They would kill me with the sword and hang her if we did not couple.

I puzzled over this. Why would they give me a woman and expect me to join with her? Prisoners were not often treated this nicely, I told myself, almost smiling at my thought. The girl, however, did not smile. She said something in her own language. Tears edged her pleading eyes. She did not want to die. She knew it would cost us our lives if we did not do what we expected of us. Then, out of desperation, she pulled the smock she was wearing over her head, threw it at my feet, and stood there, showing her beautiful body with its smooth lines, finely shaped breasts, and delicate red hair at the juncture of her thighs. She took my hand and tugged urgently.

I had been at sea and away from women for months. The girl's presence worked its spell. I disrobed and lay down with her.

Straw crackled as we settled onto the bed. Dust rose from the coarsely-made mattress. She spread her legs so her feet rested on the end beams of the bed and tilted her bottom up. I took her in my arms. When I pushed into her, I felt resistance that gave way after only a moment. She was a virgin. She gasped in pain but then put her arms around me. We rolled. The bed creaked. More dust rose. After the pain she felt from the loss of her maidenhead passed, she responded in a simple, unaffected (though inexperienced) manner. After a minute or so, she gasped and squealed in amazed pleasure. After only a short time, I emptied my seed into her and we were still. When I rolled off, I saw she had bled.

I stood. Sorrow and guilt came over me. An image of Janisa appeared in my mind. I looked down at the girl. She lay in bed twisting a stand of hair. I had just pulled on my trousers when the door burst open. Two old women bustled in. Ignoring me, they converged on the woman with whom I had just coupled. She started to sit up but they put their hands on her and spoke. She settled back on the mattress. One of them said something to her. She spread her legs. The women examined her intimacy, rubbed her hymeneal blood on their fingers, sniffed it, tasted it, smiled, nodded, and clucked in approval. The girl smiled back sheepishly, as if proud that she had done what was required of her correctly. They helped her up and gently put a blanket around her. I had not noticed, but the solemn woman in the red cloak stood by the open door. She must have watched the examination. The two old women escorted the girl outside. The solemn woman stepped away. The door closed once again.

I finished dressing and sat down on the bed. They had fed me and given me a woman. I once more felt shame for having embraced her, though it had been the right thing to do. She could not have been more than fifteen or sixteen. Her being a virgin sent my mind back to my wedding night. It was exactly what I had felt with Janisa. I remembered taking her in my arms, pressing into her warm nest, feeling that resistance, and then feeling it give away and hearing her gasp in joy and pain. Janisa was dead. Lark and Tessa, my two young daughters, were dead as well. Even if they were not dead, I would likely never get out of this place to see them again. I sat down on the bed and wept at the bitter blow Fate had dealt me. I sobbed as the pain of all I had lost swept over me, soaking me like rain. I lay down and dozed. I woke with a start when I sensed someone lying next to me. The girl. Warm, sweet, smiling in the safety of my presence, she pressed her body against mine. They had washed her (I could smell soap) and dressed her in white smock. I smiled at her and once more drifted off to sleep.

Four weeks later she would tell me she was pregnant.

II

A rooster's crow awoke me. The girl was gone. I relieved myself in the chamber pot. The door opened. The girl came in with two large wooden bowls filled with hot porridge. Eyes bright, an expression of hope and optimism on her face, she held them up. We sat on the edge of the bed. She gave me a bowl and lifted hers to her lips. I did the same, sipping the thick gruel. She smiled. I set the bowl on in my lap and pointed to myself.

"Aschel," I said.

She gazed at me a moment and then understood.

"Brenna," he said, pointing at herself. Again, she pointed with her thumb, not with her finger. I indicated the porridge, the bowl, and her garment and learned they were *brunyon*, *scala* and *qwisk*, respectively. She said, *gurek*, pointing to herself. I eventually learned this meant *wife*.

I spent the morning trying to get an idea of what their language was like. As a trader, I had developed a knack for getting other nations' speech. The tongue they spoke here was simpler than the ones spoken in the southern seas near the Mayan realms, more what the men who lived in Vineland and Labrador spoke. Structurally, the languages of the north were more logical, and less poetic than those of the Mayan world where I traded goods frequently. I had long spoken Latin, the language of the most powerful kingdom in Europa. I had the idea I hand wandered on to the northern limits of that continent. The Latin and the language these people spoke were faintly similar. I sensed I was in a more remote portion of that land mass, in the colder reaches, not near the southern sea that the Roman kingdom spread around.

Brenna patiently taught me words. She had bright intelligent eyes, and her gestures were animated and energetic. As always, being near her made me remember my wife, so that whatever pleasure I derived from Brenna's presence had a cloud over it. After she had told me the meanings of dozens of words, the door opened. She gazed up uneasily as two stern-faced men beckoned me to come outside. They led me out. She followed at a distance, hands folded in front of her.

I walked past trees to a beach. A fresh, salt breeze blew in my face. Birds sang and gulls circled in the bright, blue sky. People stood all about. It looked as if the entire village had assembled. I saw faces I recognized: the Chieftain, the tall woman and her servant girls (a priestess and her acolytes, I saw now), the man who was hostile to me yesterday. Feet planted in the sand, they gazed at me with curiosity. I sensed less hostility in their looks, though I was not certain I could read their expressions exactly. My escorts led me to a grassy spot. One of them handed me a sword. The hostile villager, the one with black hair, approached me, his sword at ready. The villagers formed a circle. I understood this would be a trial by combat, a custom widely practiced in Europa.

Fear gripped me, but I gathered my courage and resolution. I had been trained in the arts of war and had fought for my life in sea battles and once against the Azteca. Back home on my island, I excelled at sword drill and sword juggling. Despair suggested I give up and not resist—let this villager kill me and have it done with. Hopelessness at my loss of homeland and family made me think it might be better just to die. But I dismissed these thoughts. I would give him a good fight and hope for the best. My opponent advanced on me in a way that indicated he was a skilled, experienced fighter. I held up one hand. He stopped. I looked at the village leader, pointed to my sword, and held up two fingers. He blinked in puzzlement. I pointed to the sword and then to my empty hand. He understood, though he seemed surprised. They gave me a second blade.

In Atlantis we fight with two swords—a technique that gives us an advantage and often frightens off attackers. I had excelled at sword-fighting as a boy and could handle a blade well enough to do tricks at parties. I weighed the weapons in my hands and nodded. The tribal leader said something. I saw the Brenna standing at the edge of the crowd, her eyes wide with fear. The combat began.

Growling and swinging wildly, the dark-haired man charged me. I dodged him, parrying a close swing with one of my blades and forcing his blade down into the soft dirt. I might have slain him immediately, but I saw the smirks on the faces of the onlookers, especially the men. This was a warrior culture that admired *bravado* and posturing by men of arms. I planned my strategy accordingly.

He came at me again. This time I stood my ground and fought him head-on—the most dangerous phase of our combat. He was strong and quick and could flourish his sword with amazing alacrity. I focused my attention and deflected his thrusts. The blades rang in the calm morning sunshine. After ten minutes of close fighting, sweat streaming from our bodies, we backed off to rest.

Brenna stood alone, though not far from a klatch of girls her age. She looked anxious (she did not want to become a widow after one day of marriage), but her blue eyes were also excited and full of pride.

After we got our breath, he came at me again, lifting his sword high, running at a crouch. I could see he meant to leap on me. When he sprang—he was strong and jumped high—I dove under his feet, rolled, sprang up and stabbed him in the left buttock.

The crowd roared with laughter. A few people applauded and whistled. My assailant turned but fell down. This got another laugh. He limped a couple of steps toward me and then fell to one knee. The leader of the tribe spoke in a loud voice, came over, and put his left hand on my head, his right hand in the air. I had won. The crowd cheered. Brenna squealed and leaped up and down.

I thought it was over but (I was told later when I could speak the language) custom dictated that when one was bested in a trial by combat, a kinsman could challenge the winner. The kinsman was a boy, possibly sixteen years old. He ran at me, wildly swinging, cursing and roaring. I hit one of my blades on the ground, which distracted him, swung the other sword, and flipped his weapon out of his hand into the air. I would defeat this opponent with finesse, I thought. I threw my two blades up, caught his when it came down, and began to juggle the three swords.

Sword juggling was an art in Atlantis, but was also used to teach dexterity to boys learning how to fight. I had always been good at it and juggled at parties to amuse girls. I threw the three swords from my combat here up into the air and caught them, amazing the crowd and my opponent. I decided on a dangerous maneuver we called "the waterwheel." Rather than catching the swords and throwing them up and down, I spun them so they whorled in front of me like a waterwheel. I only did so for a few seconds. If one spun off it could kill me or, worse, someone in crowd—the move had been outlawed in Atlantis. I tossed the three swords up and slapped their hilts as they fell so they punched into the soil, forming a triangle around me. I bowed.

The villagers stood in silence a moment and then burst into wild jubilation (except for the man I had wounded and the boy I had humiliated). The cheering went on and on. The chieftain walked over and clasped my hand. He nodded over to Brenna, who came scurrying up and threw her arms around me.

"*Bennath*," she whispered repeatedly. *Bennath* means *blessing*. I would later come to understand why she said this.

The people crowded around me. They gave me a stein of fermented drink, slapped at me (a friendly gesture, I assumed) and expressed best wishes. Though I could not understand, I could judge their tone and read the expressions on their faces.

After that, they gave me freedom to walk the village. It lay bounded on one side by thick forest and on the other side by the sea. Larger than it appeared because most of the houses were hidden in the woods, it held about three-hundred people. Five other villages nearby were allies and part of the larger clan.

I worked hard on the language. I constantly asked Brenna the meaning of words. By listening to conversations and sitting in as their bards and storytellers spoke, I began to learn how their speech functioned — verbs, tenses, gender and voice. At the end of three months, I could speak their tongue well enough engage in simple conversations and find out where I had come to dwell and what the village that sheltered me was like.

I was in the land of the Britons, a land the Romans called Albion, White Island. The Romans, the villagers told me, had seized parts of their island and seemed to have their eyes on this territory now. When I told them I had traded with Romans and spoke their language, they were astonished and said Freya, the goddess they worshipped, had sent me their way to perform a miracle that might save them. A valiant, capable fighter, and one who spoke the Latin tongue, I could negotiate with the Roman commander who had established a camp some forty miles from here. Rowena, I was told, did not converse with men because she was a virgin and a pledged woman. I had no alternative but to agree.

It would be less complicated now that Atlantis had either sunk beneath the sea or been severely damaged by a tidal wave. The hostilities that had been escalating between us and the Romans would have abruptly ended.

That night, on the straw mattress, Brenna asleep beside me, I remembered Janisa.

The walled cities of Atlantis, with their opulent houses, tree-lined boulevards, theaters, and sports arenas, held millions of beautiful women. I always fancied I had found the most beautiful of them all. I would never have had a chance to win her except I became an unexpected hero at the battle of Chasca.

Chasca was a trading port we established on the coast of the Western Continent. We negotiated with the locals, paid them a yearly fee for the use of the place, and named it for one of their goddesses, Chasca, the Maiden of the Sun. They brought a priestess of their goddess to conduct worship there. We built a temple for them. Before they installed the priestess, however, they said we had to provide them with a "temple maiden" to attend the priestess.

Atlantis was not a religious society. We believe in the Fates, though no one thought they were actual entities. To enjoy favor from the Fates you behaved morally—you lived up to the moral codes we had established. And that was it. Religion went no further than that. We did not have temples or worship.

Our leaders, who wanted the port to be established, agreed to send young women to serve the Priestess of Chasca. Chasca was a virgin goddess, so the girls serving had to be pure. Women from wealthy families were asked to go. Chasca throve as a trading post. We brought steel weapons and farm tools and traded them for fruit, produce, gold, gemstones, and medicinal herbs. Chasca established itself as a wealthy trading port and stood for two-hundred years.

The temple girls served three years. After a while, it became quite an honor and an adventure for young women to do a stint as a temple maiden in the exotic wilds of the Western Continent before marrying. Only the most beautiful and accomplished girls got the prize. Janisa won the spot easily.

I was in Chasca the day she arrived. When she stepped off the Atlantian passenger ship, I gasped in amazement at her beauty, and dignity, but also at the look of playfulness and irony in her eyes. After selling my cargo at a good profit, I attended a twilight ceremony (open to the public) where the native priestess received her as an acolyte. I was astonished when Janisa spoke to me at the reception afterwards.

I was drinking wine and chatting with a group of native Nakbe men (I had learned their language to a fair degree of competency). We had, in fact, been swapping dirty jokes when they fell silent and looked uneasy. I turned and saw her, a glass of wine held in her long fingers.

The Nakbe, who viewed her as a consecrated maiden they could not look upon — let alone speak with — politely bowed and melted into the crowd.

"I hope I didn't scare them off," she said.

I laughed. "To them, you are a temple maiden dedicated to Chasca. Even looking at your for too long can bring her wrath on a man."

"You speak their language admirably. How did you learn it?"

"I'm a merchant. I deal with them a lot and have picked up their speech over the course of the last few years." Then I added, "A good beginning, and the work's half done."

I said this in Kev, a dialect spoken along

the north coast of Atlantis, where I grew up. I would not normally have spoken in dialect to someone I did not know (it would have been considered rude), but her beauty had knocked me a bit off keel. She wore a long-sleeved white dress that fell in pleated folds to her ankles, gold sandals, and an onyx bracelet on her left arm. Her dark brown hair, tied up with gold ribbons, framed her round face with its green eyes and small mouth and nose, which gave her an impish expression. The proverb I quoted seemed glib given the sanctity her presence communicated. I opened my mouth to apologize and translate, but her lips bent into a smile and opened.

"It's good to hear the language I speak each day and to hear it on the other side of the world," she said.

We spent the next half hour conversing in Kev. Other Atlantians gathered around us to puzzle and try to move the conversation (and her) to the official dialect of our nation, but she would return to conversing in our exotic tongue.

I found out about her. She was Janisa from the family Ashton. When I heard this, I almost dropped my wine. The Ashton family owned the ships, the shipbuilding industry, the warehouses, and most of the property in the province I hailed from. We had more wine. I was startling to get drunk. When a band of Atlantians the governor had cobbled together began to play music, I looked up at her. I was too afraid to ask, but she said, "I'd be delighted," and held out her hand.

We danced. Finally, she graciously excused herself to dance with other men. I was bold enough and foolish enough kiss her on the cheek.

"I'll make that the last kiss I have in three years. I will officially 'enter' the Temple when the moon, Na Tuva, rises in half an hour. After that, I'm completely off-limits to men. You didn't have my last dance for the next three years, but you had my last kiss."

I went home that night in love with her.

Being a merchant, I was practical and knew how to recognize liabilities. Her family would think me less than nothing. And besides, she would be cloistered for the next three years. What had seemed like the beginning a formulaic fairy tale where the poor boy marries the princess would go no further than the unexpected dance.

I did see her once. I was at Chasca during the Festival of the Sun, when the priestess and her acolyte could talk to the public. I had put into port eighteen months after first meeting Janisa. The intervening time had been tough, full of storms and a fight with pirates. I had made a profit on most of my ventures, though, and invested them well so I had more money than I had ever had. Still, I didn't get my hopes up about Janisa. She might not even remember or recognize me, I thought, as I got ready to go the banquet.

To my surprise, delight, and rue, she came over and spoke to me in Kev.

"We can only talk," she said. "You can't

touch me." Then she looked both ways and whispered, "Damn it."

We talked and drank wine.

"Is it fun?" I asked. "I mean being an acolyte?"

"'Fun' isn't the right word. It's... *interesting*. Ixanti is devoted to her goddess. It's sad she will live her whole life as a priestess and never marry. She is a beautiful woman—beautiful inside and out. I'm glad the religion we have doesn't shut up women like that."

We conversed for an hour. She went off to talk to other guests. I left for parts north. Despite her friendliness, I doubted it would go beyond these little chats. In a year, she would return home. Her family would have plans for her. They would marry her off to a wealthy businessman or a rich politician.

When I came back to Chasca the third time, I saved her life.

When returned to trade goods I had acquired in Vineland, the city was in garrison. Tribes from the north, the governor told me, had begun to attack the native settlements. These new tribes were well-organized, possessed sophisticated weapons, and used skillful battle tactics. They also practiced human sacrifice. Many of the locals had fled to the lands south of Chasca at their advance. There had been talk of abandoning the port.

I went to bed that night. The blare of alarm trumpets ended my sleep. As I dressed and armed, I heard shouting, screaming, war cries, the clanking of sword on sword. I smelled smoke. When I ran into the night, my heart froze in fear. Chasca was burning. The attackers had gotten inside. This would be a fight for our very lives.

I got my swords out and joined the fray. They fought with spears and throwing sticks. Our forces had driven their vanguard toward the battered-in gate, but the enemy tribes yielded slowly. The ground beneath my feet was wet with blood. One of the enemy tribesmen sprang out to engage me. He swung a club embedded with razor-sharp shards of black glass. I parried and used two swords to my advantage, driving him closer and closer to a burning building near the main fight. As the flames grew hotter on his back, he made a desperate lung at me. I took of his left arm then his head. As he fell, I heard a shriek of agony—a woman screaming in terror and pain, her voice then fading.

Stepping over the enemy I had just killed, I followed the noise. Going down an alley beside the burning building, I came to a square surrounded by trees. I remembered it was some sort of sacred garden only the priestess and her acolyte could enter. The firelight flared. I saw Ixanti lying on the ground. She was naked, splashed with blue paint, and I saw a blood-soaked gash below her breasts. Her eyes stared up in sightless terror. Blood oozed from the wound and from a corner of her mouth. Three men stood over her. One held an object in his cupped hands. Blood dripped through his fingers. I realized an instant and shock and revulsion that he held her heart. They had cut out her heart and were offering it to a deity.

I shouted—not a challenge as much as a reaction to the atrocity I had stumbled upon. They turned, startled. When they did so, I saw, behind them, held fast by a muscled soldier, the pale figure of Janisa.

Eyes wide, mouth open, she looked mad with terror. They had stripped her too and poured blue paint over her head and shoulders. She was next.

Instinct, rage, and love possessed me like a demon. As the enemy warriors rushed at me, I screamed and raced to meet them, swinging my two swords. My senses simultaneously erased and sharpened (the only way I can express it) by the thought of Janisa having her heart cut out. I felt contact, heat, and heard the ringing of metal. I smelled the foulness of human stench, heard curses and screams—then silence.

I stood, confused by the sudden silence, over three bodies. I had killed them all. The one holding Janisa put a glass knife to her throat, stared at me a moment, and then threw down the knife and fled.

I did something my military instructors told me never to do. I dropped one of my swords and threw the other at the retreating man. It whooshed through the air, end over end, and hit him square between the shoulder blades. As he crumpled, I rushed over to Janisa.

She was incoherent with terror, trembling and gasping for air. I lowered her to the ground, tore the cape off the man who had offered Ixanti's heart to the sky, and threw the garment over Janisa. I spoke to her, telling her she was safe and I would protect her. She nodded to indicate she understood, calmed down, and breathed more evenly. I pulled another garment off a dead soldier and covered Ixanti's body.

By now the attack had been repulsed. The enemy had fled into the jungle I took a double handful of water from a fountain in the garden and gently poured it over Janisa's face. She opened her eyes and looked at me. She seemed coherent once more. She reached her arms out, put them around my neck, and began to sob.

I rolled on the straw mattress and tried to get comfortable. Brenna lay beside me, her breathing even and calm. As the straw in the mattress rustled, I thought of the soft bed, the perfumed sheets, and the cedar-paneled bedroom with a sky window so we could see the stars — the bed Janisa and I shared. We had shared it for eight years as husband and wife.

III

Winter is harsh and long in these northern climes. Harvest rolled around. The people in the village stored grain, dried vegetables and fish, hunted for game, sewed thick, warm clothes, and insulated houses (I would call them huts) with straw for winter's onset.

By now I knew the language well enough to speak with villagers. They seemed to like me. From Brenna I learned more about the situation in which the Fates had set me down.

First off, Brenna was a slave captured in a raid on an adjacent tribe. The Priestess of Freya, named Rowena, had wanted her for an acolyte so she was not raped or forced to serve as a whore.

When I arrived, many thought I was a Roman. The design of my boat suggested as much. Others said I was a god. After a long debate, Rowena proposed giving me a woman. If I were a god, the coupling would destroy her. If she survived, this would establish my identity as a mortal. In addition, a trial by combat could determine if I were a Roman spy. After I passed the trail by combat, they would accept me into the village and Brenna would be my wife.

Rowena fascinated me. Dignified, a pledged woman like Ixanti, she exuded such beauty I found it difficult not to stare at her. As the priestess of Freya, she had as much power as Gavin, the chief of the tribe. Because she could speak Latin, in my early days there I got most of my information on the life of the village from her.

I had picked up Latin during the times I traded goods with Romans in garrisons on the coast of Spain and Gaul. Once, when a storm trapped me in a settlement in Vineland and I ended up staying there three months, I studied it with the Christian monks who took me in as a guest. Latin was the language of their religion, even though they spoke the Norse tongue day to day. I had developed a fluency in it because of late I had sailed quite a bit on the coast and dealt with the Romans. Rowena's tribal elders had given her to the Roman temple in Londinium when she was four in an exchange to seal a treaty. A Roman family adopted her and later took her to Sicily. At age eighteen, she vowed that if the goddess Freya would enable her to get home, she would devote herself to her service.

Freya had provided a way.

"The thing we are concerned about is the intentions of the Romans," she said. "They want the tin mines further up country. They have offered us terms of peace—our freedom for the use of the mines—but we are not certain we can trust them."

"Why not?"

"They have enslaved the rest of the island. We fear they will do the same to us. They never conquered our lands because they saw nothing of value here. Now they want the mines. We are uneasy."

Snow soon covered the land. Quiet fell. Brenna grew. She would pull up her garment and proudly show me her stomach. "It is a boy," she said eagerly. "I know I will bear you a son." The other young women in the village accepted her now, gave her status as a wife and, it was whispered, one upon whom rested the favor of the Holy Priestess Rowena.

I worked hard with the other men, fishing through holes in the ice, hunting in the vast, snowy forest, cutting wood, hauling water, shoveling snow. Harvest had been good. There was plenty of food and beer. The bards sang in Gavin's hall at night. Wolves howled in the small hours. Winter wore on at its long pace.

Everyone kept telling me our child would be a boy. The midwives said Brenna's stomach was curved with the curve of a male child. I had never had a son, though Janisa and I had planned to have more children. My two little girls— beautiful, innocent angels—had died in the sinking. The thought of their terrified last moments, when the ground rumbled, shifted and then collapsed into the sea, drove me to distraction so much that when it entered my mind I had to divert my thinking. Probably they had died quickly. Still, terror and pain would have enveloped their delicate bodies and their sweet souls, if only for a few moments.

It had happened with the Westward Isles forty years ago. They had sunk into the depths with grievous loss of life. Those islands had served as a staging area for our planned conquest of Europa. The early stages of the campaign had gone well, I had read, and then suddenly ended. The Europeans were puzzled. Our Western Islands had disappeared, but by the time I came on the scene, no one was concerned the same thing might happen to the prime islands. Atlantis

Main was larger and more stable than the Westward Islands. It could not sink, people said. Plans for a new campaign began. The government enlisted my help because I spoke the Roman language.

I had encountered them already. They traded with the Northmen and sent vessels along the Gallic coast and to the island chains that lie a distance from Europa. I sometimes exchanged goods with them. When the first naval clashes began, the Romans arrested and imprisoned me. My basic knowledge of Latin turned to idiomatic fluency in this time. Soon I found myself working as an intermediary between the Romans and my own people. I parlayed and carried documents between the two parties. More than once, I shipped diplomats to neutral locations (Iceland and the Faroe Islands) for negotiations. War seemed inevitable—until one of the potential belligerents disappeared into the watery abyss.

The Atlantian politicians had been confident they could capture territory in Europa. They had set their eyes on Hispaniola and the White Island (where I now found myself living). I was not so sure my nation could have taken those territories. I had feared a reversal and envisioned red-cloaked Romans raising their gold eagle standards in the main square of Atlantis City, our capitol. The Romans were a single-minded, efficient machine, and I never thought my people could outlast them in a long war.

Of course, it did not matter now.

As spring came, harsh and rough, to the land where I now lived, Brenna began to feel the child coming. She went into labor. Unlike in Atlantis, where physicians delivered children and men were kept away, I was present, holding her hand while the women of the village coaxed her through the process. She felt pain to be sure, but Brenna was young and strong and gave birth easily. It was a son, as she had predicted. I watched with amazement as the child emerged, pale and wan, and then turned pink and healthy after the chief midwife pinched him and he cried. The midwife gave him to me. I held him, trying not to think of my girls, smiled, kissed him, then gave him to Brenna, who looked weary but elated. She gave him her breast and he began to suck.

The child, whom we named, Balder, grew strong and demanding. Brenna was up and around the next day and more or less assumed her routine duties within a week—albeit, dragging a baby around with her.

After a month, the two of us went to see Rowena to receive the child's charm name.

Rowena lived outside the village. Her home was a sacred place, so no one came there without a summons. Brenna carried Balder. She seemed fearful—not of Rowena, but of the fact that she represented the gods and the power of the supernatural. My wife wore an embroidered dress and boots (she usually went barefoot, even in winter). She had braided her hair. I wore a tunic, a kilt Brenna had woven for me, and boots.

One of the acolytes admitted us and led us to what Brenna called "the goddess chamber." A circular room with a stone floor, it encompassed perhaps twenty feet. A wooden image of the goddess Freya stood at one end. She was naked and held out a sprig of holly in one hand and bowl of water in the other—both symbols of fertility. Two torches illumined the room.

We knelt. Brenna held the squirming Balder, who had begun to cry, close to her breast. The temple was a strange, quiet place full of odd smells and exuding an aura of disturbing holiness even our little child could sense. Rowena came in a moment later.

Brenna prostrated herself, holding Balder out on her bent elbows. I remained on my knees. Rowena regarded me a moment and then bent down and took up our child.

"Stand, both of you," she said. "We all stand in the presence of the goddess."

Brenna rose. I followed. We faced the image. Rowena fell silent a long time.

"His secret name is Calin," she said. "This will shield him from curses and the evil eye."

Another long moment passed.

"The blessing of goddess be up on you," she said.

"The blessing of the goddess fall sweetly," Brenna murmured, repeating what sounded like a liturgical formula.

Rowena gave Balder back to Brenna.

"A beautiful child," she said.

"Thank you, my lady," Brenna replied, looking down, her voice full of pious deference. Rowena smiled, not scornfully but lovingly and tenderly for my bride's unaffected reverence.

"I need to speak to your husband," she said.

Brenna bowed, our child in her arms. Surprised by the request, I went to her, kissed her and kissed my son's head. He cooed. Brenna took him out.

Silence fell. I stood facing Rowena—a beautiful, strong, striking figure of a woman. I would guess her age at over thirty. Her hair, braided and wound around her head, glowed its brown-blonde in the lamplight of the room. Like many of the women I had seen here, she had a squarish face. Her large blue eyes and sensitive mouth charmed me. She looked at me with the restrain and decorum demanded of a priestess, but in her eyes I saw vulnerability and maybe even humor and irony.

"*Vestri uxor est a decorus mulier.*"[1]

Somehow I sensed she wanted to speak on more than an official level. I spoke what I felt in my heart.

"*Is est a parvulus.*"[2]

"*Have vos been matrimonium pro?*"[3]

"I had a wife," I answered as we continued

---

[1] Your wife is a beautiful woman.
[2] She is a child.
[3] Have you been married before?

in Latin. "We were married eight years. We had two children—daughters. They perished in the flood."

"I'm sorry. You speak of the flood. You are Atlantian?"

I looked up suddenly, surprised she knew of the existence of Atlantis.

"I know it is a real place," Rowena said.

"Many believe it to be mythical."

"I know it is real. I've been there."

I stared at her.

"Let us retire to my rooms. It is unseemly to be chatting leisurely in the presence of the goddess."

She clapped her hands. One of her acolytes came in and bowed. Rowena spoke to her. She turned. Rowena gestured for me to follow.

We walked through a long corridor to a room lit with torches. A table occupied the center. She invited me to sit and took her place across from me. The acolyte, whom she called Onela, disappeared and returned carrying an earthenware pitcher and two ceramic glasses, which she set before us and filled. I smelled the fragrance and saw the deep red color. My heart filled with delight. Wine. Rowena lifted her glass.

"May I propose a toast?"

I raised my glass in response.

"To your family and sweet little Brenna, and to your son. May blessings find all three of you. And to our village—may it prosper and be free."

We drank. The wine tasted strong, full, and bracing. I put down my glass.

"Marvelous."

"Wine is hard to come by in these parts," Rowena said. "The people here are beer drinkers and don't have the patience to tend vines. Merchants buy it from the Romans and deliver it to me."

"I appreciate your efforts to obtain it." I hesitated but, again, sensing her desire to communicate, I went on, "When I came to your shore, I had phial of wine I had been saving. I planned to drink it before I died. I thought I might as well go out of this life with the taste of a good vintage in my mouth. In the confusion of my capture, I forgot about it."

"I have it. We found it on the boat. It's in the goddess's treasury. I will return it to you. You thought we were going to kill you?"

"I had ample reason to believe as much."

She faintly smiled. "Perhaps you did. I'm sure, given the resplendent world from whence you came, you thought you had landed in a republic of savages."

"If I thought that, experience has altered my perception." When she did not reply, I asked, "How did you come to Atlantis?"

"On a diplomatic mission. But first tell me what became of your civilization."

"It sank into the sea," I answered. Sadness and grief over my family made me pause a moment. "All perished. I am a merchant. I was out in my ship in sight of land. We had just left harbor but were becalmed. My crew boarded our skiff to pull at the oars and get us away from land before the tide came in. We heard rumbling. The sky went black and the land sank. The sinking raised a massive tidal wave. My crew went under. The wave tossed my ship like a leaf in a stream, but by a miracle it survived and rode the crest of the wave. I actually saw the island go under. Then wind and tsunami drove me north. Here I am."

"When I was nineteen," Rowena returned, "my guardian took me to your sadly perished land. My foster father, Horatius Germanicus Glacialis, served in the diplomatic corps."

"You say your 'foster father.'"

"I am from this land, though my ancestors were Frisians who settled here long ago. At age six, the tribes made a pact with the Romans and I was given as a... well, a hostage of sorts. Glacialis adopted me. He renamed me Drusilla. I was pledged to be a Temple maiden in Londinium, but the Temple of Vesta was too small to board the priestesses, so we lived at home and served our days as fire-guardians there. Eight years later the government transferred Glacialis to a post in Sicily, and I spent the rest of my youth in Rome. Caesar chose my father to accompany a party of diplomats from Rome to Atlantis. He brought me along as a scribe and so I could secure documents. Since I was a vestal, no men could speak with me or approach my dwelling, so any secret correspondence was safe with me."

"Do you remember much about it?"

"How could I forget? I had been to Rome, but I never saw such buildings and gardens as I saw in Atlantis Prime. I was dazzled."

"Atlantis Prime was the most magnificent place on earth."

"We wanted to avoid war. While negotiations went on, the citizens of your capital showed me great kindness and showered me with gifts. I still have some of them."

In the language of the village, she told Onela to fetch her container of artifacts. Once she had set it on the table. Rowena opened it.

Jewelry and crystal filled the box. It reminded me of Janisa. One object Rowena held up—an opal on a silver chain—brought tears to my eyes. I could not stop them. It was identical to a necklace Janisa owned—one she would wear when we made love. In my mind I saw her lying on the purple sheet of our bed, body white and naked, the pendant opal glimmering just above her breasts.

"I'm sorry these things bring back bad memories," Rowena said.

"They bring back good memories," I said, recovering my composure.

She had Onela take them away. I had also noticed, amid Rowena's collection of Atlantian artifacts, a small image of Chasca.

"You were an adopted daughter in an obviously prominent Roman household. How did you come here? You were a vestal. How did you come to be a priestess of Freya?"

"When the conquest of this area began, the Roman governor ordered me returned. My family was grief-stricken. I was twenty-five and they had raised me as their daughter from age six. My mother was inconsolable. My father appealed to Caesar, but diplomacy overruled family concerns. Since I was already a temple girl and a pledged virgin, the town made me a priestess of Freya. I exchanged one goddess for another. I am thirty winters old now."

I did not know what to say. I caught, though, the sadness in her eyes. I also saw a spark of determination and fire.

"As a child I was pledged to Vesta, who is a pure goddess. I was expected to be pure myself. I accepted it until I came of age. I petitioned to be freed from my vow. My petition was granted."

"But" —I was afraid but went on— "you are still a pledged woman. Is this not so?"

"It is so. But remember Freya is not a virgin goddess like Vesta or Diana. She is the goddess of childbirth and fertility and the wife of Odin. She has children. As a priestess, I hold my virgin state in potentiality."

"What does that mean?"

"It means that I guard the temple in my purity and innocence. When our community is in need, the power of Freya must be unleashed. You seem capable of logic, Aschel. If my virginity is the thing that holds the power of Freya in potentiality, you can discern, I think, what would release that potentiality."

My faculty for logic took a moment to kick in. When I realized what she was getting at, my eyes grew round with shock and astonishment. She smiled.

"I see you realize what I am announcing to you."

"Announcing?"

"Yes. This is not a request. It is a duty to which you must give yourself."

"I'm a married man," I sputtered. "You just blessed my son."

"Brenna will understand."

"Brenna"—the enormity of it stopped me. I organized my thoughts and went on. "She is only a girl—a loving, trusting girl, as gentle as anyone I've ever met. I can't hurt her by doing something like this."

"Do you love Brenna?"

The question stopped me. Logical and direct, it swept away the confusion of emotion I felt and went to the center of what she perceived was the real issue at hand. I quieted.

"Is that really an issue?"

"It is."

I looked into her blue eyes.

"It would be an act of cruelty to hurt her. I've entered into a covenant of marriage with her. It would be unethical and malicious to violate that covenant. It would constitute betrayal. It would inflict pain on an innocent, gentle soul."

"You are a kind man—kind and thoughtful. Your kindness is the result of cultivation. You came from a society where people discuss such considerations and there is discourse on matters of right and wrong. Here it is not so."

"Perhaps what you say is true. But I feel the way I feel because of the influences you correctly identify."

"Tell me about you first wife."

I could not answer right away.

"What was her name?" Rowena prompted.

"Janisa."

"You had children?"

"Two girls. Lark and Trella."

"I am sorry for your loss. Tell me about Janisa. Start with how you met."

Sadness settled over me like the weight of the ocean. After a long silence, I began to speak. I told her about our first conversation at the Port of Chasca and how I later saved her from becoming a human sacrifice. She listened closely. I told her about going to meet her father after the Azteca overran the area and we had to abandon all our trading posts.

Janisa's father, Martoza, held as much wealth as anyone on my side of Atlantis.

"Name your reward, boy," he said.

He thought I would ask for money. I stood in his resplendent guest hall, in front of his servants and the many high-ranking guests he had invited. I licked my lips and gathered my courage.

"I want Janisa's hand in marriage," I said. A stunned silence descended. Everyone held his breath. The very flames in the lamps seemed not to flicker. After a moment, a crooked smile came to his lips.

"Surely you jest," he said.

"No, sir. I do not jest. I want to marry your daughter. I love her."

A dark look of anger came to his eyes, but then he seemed to remember that I had saved her from a horrible death.

"I remember from what she has told me that you two do know each other and like each other. But let's be realistic. You come from different parts of our society. Youthful infatuations arise, I know. I think, if you were married, you would soon find your differences are greater than you imagine. I do not want my child unhappily married—or, for that matter, you, Aschel. I am asking you to put romantic considerations aside and try to view this whole thing more realistically."

"I understand, my lord. I propose you ask Janisa how she feels about it. I will be governed by her reply."

This satisfied him. He thought my proposal the result of my folly or my desire to marry into his wealth. His daughter, he assumed, would concur with his judgment. When Janisa said she also loved me and wanted to be my wife, it must have come as a shock to him.

He did, to his credit, keep his word and, after Janisa and I were married, accepted me, and eventually became a friend and confidant. He had loved our little girls with such starry-eyed doting I could hardly keep my composure when I recalled it.

"She was beautiful and educated?" Rowena asked.

"Both of these things—and passionate and loving."

My mind wandered to our wedding night. The ceremony was long and tiring. A banquet kept us up late. But when we went to the chamber, it was as if the very floodgates of passion opened for us. I remember how desire seized her and how she moaned and gasped in delight that very first time. We made love all that night and all the next day. Because of Janisa's high social standing, guests, including the King and Queen of Atlantis, came to call on us our first week together. They brought expensive gifts. We politely entertained them, then, when they were gone, sprinted to the bedroom.

Remembering drained me of strength. "I'm sure your wife was a virgin, as I am. Were there other women in your life?"

Her question—and its directness—startled me so much I gave the answer with my reaction alone. No point in trying to lie, as I had already told the truth with my eyes.

"You are a sailor and a merchant. I understand. We often sailed great distances. My father, who was a good man and loved my mother, availed himself of the services women in ports offered; or, he traveled with a woman he had hired from the guild of prostitutes. Being away from my mother, deprived of her affection and her embrace, he needed release. I don't think less of him, or of you, for that matter. You are a man and must find release periodically. But you have had other women as partners?"

"Yes—but not after I married Janisa."

"It was of necessity, and so is this. It must be soon. The Romans are sending patrols into the forest to scout the perimeter of our village. The power of Freya must be released at once."

"What will happen once it is released?"

"That is in the goddess's keeping. She will do as she proposed and we will see her work."

"You believe in her?"

The left side of her mouth twitched. "I have been around goddesses all my life, Aschel. I am a skeptical woman. In my education, I read the philosophers—even ones like Epicurus and Heraclitus, who were hostile to religion and did not believe in divinities. I have often doubted. But I know when I am in the presence of a deity. You may think me mad or deluded for saying this, and I won't try to change your mind about the matter. I will only say be careful how you regard divinities. They can be disagreeable."

I left and returned to my house. Brenna sat by the hearth, rocking Balder, who was fast asleep. Her left breast, smeared with milk and red from our boy's tugging, lay exposed to the flickering firelight. She smiled.

"He eats well and he is strong," she said. She pressed him to her body. I said nothing. The silence became awkward. She said, "I know what the priestess has commanded you to do."

"I don't want to betray you."

She put Balder in his crib, came over, and led me to the bed. We sat down.

"It will not be a betrayal. I know you are a faithful man. But when the gods command, we must obey."

"How do you know it is the goddess, Brenna? Maybe this is only Rowena's desire."

She looked about her, eyes dark.

"You must not say such things. The goddess will be angry. You must do what the Lady Priestess instructs you to do. We will be all the more blessed when you obey. If the Romans come, they will make us slaves. We would be sold and you would never see your son or me again. Do what the goddess orders. Do not blaspheme."

We bedded down for the night. Brenna dozed off. I could not sleep. Rowena's interrogation disturbed me. In addition, I had lied to her. I had not been faithful to Janisa. I slept with port whores and "boat whores" who would come alongside out on the water and offer their services. When I was in Vineland, I had an extended relationship with a widow. How would a liaison with Rowena be any different? In addition, this was not a liaison. Brenna knew and insisted I participate. She saw it as an act of divine service. I sighed as I lay next to her small, warm, naked body. I had no choice. Rowena was beautiful. I would have chosen her if the choice had been between her and Brenna. Still, it did not seem right.

Brenna and I made love in the morning. I went to work logging to build a new home for one of the men in the village whose family had expanded. I liked the hard work and camaraderie. Spring had been uncommonly warm. Brenna had already broken ground for a garden. Wildflowers decorated the forest with color, blazing vividly beneath the green-gold leaves emerging on the trees.

Two weeks after Rowena and I talked, I received a summons to present myself at the Temple of Freya at sunset on the eve of the new moon. That would be in two days.

I felt nervous and awkward—more so when I realized everyone in the village knew of the summons and knew what it meant. They treated me with curious deference. The men would not allow me to do heavy work. Though they would not say why, I understood. Brenna insisted we abstain from intercourse until I returned.

"You must save your vital strength," she told him.

"Is this a rule?"

"There is no rule, but it seems wise, don't you think?"

I pondered and then asked, "Does Rowena expect to get pregnant from this? Does she plan to have a child?"

Brenna stared a moment. She did not look shocked. Her expression did not suggest a reaction to blasphemy. The question seemed not to have occurred to her. It was improper and a little dangerous, in her thinking, to speculate on the designs of the goddess Freya.

"I don't know," she answered. "I suppose this is hidden in Freya's will. But if she means for Rowena to be pregnant, it will be so."

I took her to bed. She protested.

"You must save your seed and your desire."

"If it's all in the goddess's keeping, she will provide me with the strength and all the seed necessary to fulfill her purpose."

She reluctantly yielded to me. In the morning, I helped her till soil for in the garden and plant cabbage and turnips. In the afternoon, I inspected my boat. The hull was in good shape, though the sail had rotted to tatters. After the affair with Rowena ended, I thought I might take it out to sea—not to escape. That was out of the question. Where would I go? Fate had cast me here. The people had accepted me and this place was home. Still, it would be good to get away from land, to feel the familiar swell and bound of the ocean beneath my feet, to breathe the salt breeze and once more know the exhilaration of riding the back of the ocean.

The appointed day arrived. I got out of bed and looked through the front door to see Venus blaze on the dark horizon. Brenna stirred, got up, and kissed me. I walked out the door.

I was startled to see Jannet and Olena, the two acolytes who served Rowena, there. They bowed.

"We have come to escort you," Jannet said. Olena carried a wooden bowl that smoked in the morning coolness. She dipped her finger into it, reached up, and ran her index finger across my forehead. I felt something warm. Blood. They had sacrificed an animal as a prelude to what would happen soon.

"Come," Olena said.

We walked through the village common. The sky, not yet entirely dark, blazed with stars. The moon, a dark shell, barely visible, hung in the sky above the trees. The houses, quiet and dark, stood in neat rows. Newly tilled gardens, pigsties, and woodpiles lay in shadow. The three of us walked along in silence. A fox (a vixen) with two cubs scampered across our path, a streak of red against the green of trees. It startled Jannet and Olena. They gasped in surprise but quickly recovered their decorum and walked on.

Entering the temple, they knelt and recited a prayer in a language I did not understand. It was not the language the village spoke. After that, they led me to the room that lodged the image of Freya. A pallet of pillows and quilts lay on the floor. The image of the goddess gazed out at us with her outstretched hands. Olena left and returned with a ceramic cup.

"Drink this," she said—not a request, an instruction.

It was a posset, milk and wine. I drained it. Olean took the cup out and returned with Jannet.

"We will undress you," Jannet said. You must not touch your clothes or assist us in any way. You are holy to the goddess and must not compromise your sanctity."

Olena knelt and pulled off my boots. Piece by piece, she and Jannet removed my clothing. Acolyte girls were required to be virgins, but neither of the young women—I would guess their ages at fourteen or fifteen—showed embarrassment or awkwardness as they stripped me. "Wait. The Lady Priestess will soon arrive," Jannet said when they were finished and I stood bare and awkward before them. With that, the two girls exited, taking my clothing.

I gazed at the image of Freya and at the holly bob and bowl in her hands. The doors open. Rowena came in. She wore a scarlet robe. Her untied hair fell in a cascade of gold to her waist. I could see, around her neck, an opal, large, bright, its colors catching the light of the oil lamps that burned dimly in the space near the goddess's image. It was the opal necklace she had showed me earlier, the one so like what Janisa used to wear.

As she approached, I wondered if I could perform. Anxiety robs a man of the vital force it takes to make love with a woman. And I was anxious, upset over this lapse of faith with Brenna, and aware that everyone in the village knew about what I was expected to do. Failure would bring disgrace, perhaps even retribution. Still, I wondered if the fear I felt might overwhelm the natural currents of desire.

Rowena let her robe fall to the ground. She was not short and petitely roundish like Brenna, but more like Janisa — tall, with long arms and legs, a strong, flat stomach, wide, almost square breasts, powerful thighs that framed the tuft of light brown hair above her opening.

When I saw her nakedness, a current of lust tore through me and my doubts about being able to perform were laid to rest. I realized the posset was an aphrodisiac. Desire for Rowena drove every thought from my brain. I wanted to seize her, to take her in my arms and push her to ground. She put her arms around me — I felt her considerable strength — and gently bore me to the pile of bedclothes. Even in the madness that had seized me, I knew I was on my back, she kneeling. She seized my cock, bent down, and began to lick and fondle it with her lips. After a few moments of this, she lifted herself up, held my member straight, straddled me, and lowered herself. As with Janisa and Brenna, I felt resistance. This resistance, however, did not give easily. Rowena pushed. I groaned, feeling the pressure on me. The tension increased and then gave way. Rowena cried out in pain. I felt blood splash on my loins and thighs and then warmth and moisture as I penetrated her. She sank down on me, sat still moment, and then began to move.

She moved up and down in a slow, even rhythm. Her pain passed and she moved faster, her golden hair flying, her breasts jouncing, a gasping, passionate whimpering coming from her throat. I lay beneath her and twisted my hips in a counter-motion. Rowena began to babble in Latin, then in Celtic, and then in the same language her acolytes had chanted when they prayed. I felt wave after wave of pleasure as her speech then turned to ecstatic utterance. A stream of glossolalia rose musically from her throat in eerie, beautiful cadences.

Battered by joy and warmth, I felt a spot of pleasure in my coccyx that signaled climax. Rowena moved wildly above me, the music of her voice filling the room, her thighs and bottom slapping against me, her ecstatic utterances punctuated with groans, gasps, and moans of pleasure. Then she stiffened and shouted as a spasm of joy seized her. Before her shaking and crying out ended, a stinging surge of delight overpowered me, taking me out of myself and into paradisiacal happiness. I ejaculated warm streams of seed into her.

Then silence.

Rowena lifted herself and lay down next to me. Her fair skin glowed red with the aftermath of orgasm. Blood, sweat, and semen decorated the flesh about her opening as it decorated my lower body. She pressed herself against me. Both of us panted and murmured. I kissed her hair. She pulled a thick quilt over us. In the dreamy intimacy, we dropped into the oblivion pleasure gives.

When I awoke, Oleana sat on her heels beside me. Rowena was not there.

"The Lady Priestess is bathing," she said. "Jannet is in attendance upon her. When she finishes, I will bathe you."

I only blinked and glanced over at the image of Freya. Like all images of a deity, it stared out in benevolence marked with a hint of sternness. I turned back to Olena. The younger of the acolytes, she had red hair like Brenna — though, like Rowena, she was tall with a slender torso and long arms and legs. Her eyes shone bright green. She had a plain, though not unattractive, face. I had noticed before she was missing the bottom finger on her right hand.

We remained together in silence until Jannet appeared and nodded. Onela rose. "This way."

I thought of wrapping a blanket around me but decided no. The paradox of walking buck-naked beside a virgin girl pledged to serve in the temple in purity was resolved when I remembered the attitude of the society she and I lived in. Men and women bathed together in the streams. Families slept in one large room. The people here practiced modesty and admired chastity and faithfulness, yet they frankly accepted and understood the body. You bathed naked, and Olena had been instructed to bathe me, so there was no need for shame or awkwardness on her part; she knew, from the quotidian routines of growing up, what a man's body looked like. She led me to warm bath, rolled up her sleeves, and washed me with a soapy cloth. Jannet brought my clothes in, though the two girls did not dress me as they had undressed me but said they would wait for me outside the door. I got dressed and went back into the holy place. They led me to a room I had not been in before—some kind of dining room with table and chairs. Lovely as dawn, Rowena stood at the table's head.

She nodded. Her girls bowed and left the room.

"Please come and sit, Aschel," she said. "It is customary that a woman hold the chair for a man who has begun her life as a woman.'

I went over to her. She held the chair and pushed it in as I sat. I remembered Brenna doing this for me when we first ate at a table, several nights after our first time together. A tremor of shame ran through me as Rowena sat down. She rang a small hand bell. Jannet and Olena came carrying pots of cooked eggs, roast pork, and warm bread. We had beer to drink.

It was awkward. We were not married and not even lovers. Our intercourse had been a religious ceremony, which struck me as odd and unseemly. Rowena, a beautiful woman, had yielded to my embrace by divine compulsion. *Yielded*, I thought. In fact, I had yielded. I had obeyed her command as a representative of the divine.

"The goddess is pleased," Rowena said, after we had eaten in silence a long while.

"How do you know?"

"How does one know anything? The tension in my spirit is gone. I feel the presence of the goddess."

I tried to keep vulgar rejoinders from flood his mind.

"I know," she said, reading my thoughts. "What you want to suppress comes to my mind as well. The goddess knows our thoughts and our weaknesses so don't worry about offending her, Aschel."

"Do you really believe, Rowena?"

"I did not at first. Many things attributed to a god or a goddess can be explained away. All the time I was holy to Vesta, I would attribute miracles or interventions to circumstance and human action. Often, they are just that. I have learned, in living my entire life as a temple servant, that these things are not contradictory."

My mouth full of food, I did not answer. She read the question in my eyes.

"The gods control all things. If a priestess says the temple needs food and a wealthy man or woman overhears this and provides that food, this is not merely a human action. The gods placed him where he could hear and blessed him with wealth to share. When a woman in this village cannot give birth and I come, pray, and invoke the goddess, and she bears the child, I know that my presence assures her so she relaxes and by this enables her body to give forth the child. Yet the goddess is in this as well. The woman believes I am Freya's representative and exude her power—and, in a sense, I do because the woman believes. The goddess is no less operative in what happens than if she manifested herself in visible form."

"I see."

"So, yes, Aschel. I feel calm because the unrequited desire I have held inside has been satisfied. The tension in my soul calmed because I made love to you—a man I desire and a man who is virile and who satisfied my desire. Yet the goddess is in this too. What I feel is due to the physical release that came through our embrace, but that release came at Freya's command and was a manifestation of her will. I feel her presence in the satisfaction of my lust."

I sat in silence a moment, pondering what she said and then asked, "What now?"

"I don't know."

"I mean between us."

"I know you meant that, and I have to answer, I do not know. The power of Freya has been released. This has not been done in many years. The last three priestesses who served in this place lived and died in their virginity. As for us—you will come to me again—several times until the moon has gone through the full circle and is new once more."

"Brenna?"

"Brenna understands. It is you who do not understand. Go back to her today. I will summon you when I sense it is the proper time. Love Brenna—couple with her. It is not a sacrilege. But when I call you, be obedient."

She rang the bell. Olena and Jannet came to see me out.

IV

Brenna was eager to make love to me. When the sun set the day I returned from Rowena, she closed the door, got Balder to sleep, and all but pulled me into bed. After we had finished she said she had wanted to couple with me because the power of the goddess still rested on me and if we conceived a child the child would be blessed.

I went to Rowena three times before the power of the goddess released through the priestess giving her virginity manifested itself. At least this was how the villagers interpreted it.

The house of Vorthr caught on fire. Everyone rushed to fight the blaze and managed to extinguish it, but a wall of the house fell and revealed a horde of Roman coins, weapons, and garments. Brought before the assembled village, fearing he would be tortured or his children harmed, Vorthr confessed collaboration with

Romans.

As I listened, Brenna holding my arm, Vorthr told how he had met with a Roman commander who had bribed him to give information on the village and how they might most effectively attack it. They had not formulated a plan, he said. He had met with the Roman commander three times.

When he had finished, Gavin turned to Kalea, his tall, beautiful wife.

"Did you know of this?" he asked.

She lowered her gaze.

"I knew of it."

"Both of you shall die. Your children, who are innocent, will be given to other families."

Gavin drew his sword. I wondered if I would see a formal execution, but Gavin swung his sword at Vorthr, who stood still to receive the blow. He fell to the ground. Kalea wept. Two of Gavin's lieutenants tied a noose and threw it over a tree branch. They had bound Kalea's hands behind her back and were fitting the rope around her neck when Rowena appeared.

She looked stately and terrifying. She wore a scarlet garment, gold bracelets and a gold torq. Only now she had untied her hair. It fell in a cascade of thick gold over her the red of her garment. Jannet and Olena, dressed in white, stood on either side of her.

"The goddess has spoken to me," she said, stepping forward. "Kalea has confessed guilt in this matter, but as an obedient wife she concealed it from us because of love for, and deference to, her husband. Due to this, her guilt is not certain."

At a nod from Gavin, his men took the noose off and untied her hands. Rowena observed, her face impassive. Free, Kalea put her hands together and bowed. "The truth," Rowena continued, "must be determined by trial. She will be placed in the tide pool."

When Rowena said this, Kalea's eyes grew round and her face white terror. She fell to her knees.

"Rowena, please! No! I beg you!"

"This is not my doing, Kalea."

"No," she wept. "For the love of goddess, don't torture me to death."

"It is not torture and not your death. It is a trial to determine your guilt or innocence."

"No one survives the tide pool," Kalea said, crying.

"I survived it," Rowena replied, her voice stern. "It is in the hand of the goddess. Do not speak as you have spoken. You may anger her and bring a curse upon on us all."

Kalea fell silent but for her sobbing.

"Bring her to the temple. Seanna, Trevva — go with my maidens and keep watch over her, lest her desperately fordo her own life and goddess rain judgment upon us."

They nodded, their faces showing fear at Rowena's evocation of the goddess's judgment. Olena, Jannet, the two women Rowena had pressed into service, plus three armed men, followed the priestess up to the temple.

The assembly began to break up. Some men from the village dragged Vorthr's body off. He would be buried in the woods, not in the sacred burial site near the temple. Brenna looked pale. As we neared our home, I asked about the "tide pool."

"It is too terrible to speak of," Brenna answered, holding Balder close to her, "though if you order me to speak of it, I will."

I looked at her. She had tears in her eyes. I touched her shoulder.

"Are you ill, Brenna?"

"I am sorrowful," she said. "When I came here as a captive, only Kalea showed kindness to me. She gave me food and drink and kept the other women from beating me. She showed me love in my time of fear and grief."

When we were inside and Balder was quiet, she explained the tide pool.

At two o'clock the tide was full. The village assembled by the shoreline. Rowena and her party came, leading Kalea, who wept. They escorted her to an oval hole in a shelf of rock a few feet from the sea and full of water. The party stopped.

"Strip her and bind her," Rowena ordered.

Olena pulled off Kalea's garment as she obediently held her arms straight up. I admired her strong, trim body. She had given birth to four children but not lost her shape. She stood there, white and naked, still weeping, as one of the men tied her hands in front of her and Olena knelt to bind her feet. At a nod from Rowena, two men lifted her and lowered her into the hole in the rock. She sank up to her neck, the water coming just to her chin.

The crowd gazed as Kalea's teeth chattered and her eyes closed. Spring had come early this year, the people in the settlement had told me, and the water of the bay was warmer than it usually was this time of year. Still, I did not see how she could survive this ordeal. Brenna said the tide took an hour to ebb. I saw the wretched woman shiver and gasp.

We watched in silence. Gulls screamed overhead. Kalea occasionally cried out in pain. Brenna stood there, watching her friend go through the facial expressions that come with agony. However warm the water might be, Kalea was losing the battle. Her lips turned blue. She looked sleepy and lethargic. Her breathing grew labored.

Suddenly Brenna left my side and strode toward the bound, struggling woman. A gasp went up. Some men stepped forward to seize her.

"I only want to speak to her and encourage her in the name of the goddess," Brenna said. She spoke loudly so Rowena and everyone in the crowd could hear. She normally spoke so softly that her voice sounded unnatural to me. "Is this forbidden, Lady Priestess?"

Silence—then Rowena spoke.

"It is not forbidden. Only you must not touch her."

Brenna scurried over and lay down so her lips were even with Kalea's ear.

"Kalea. It's me, Brenna. Preserve your life. Kick your feet and move your legs."

At first she did not respond. I wondered if she were unconscious or perhaps even dead. But after a moment her body shook. She began to thrash and kick.

"Yes. Yes, my sister. Struggle. The goddess Hel will not receive your soul. Call on Freya, who does not desire your death. She preserved you from the noose, now she will shield your body from the cold."

Kalea thrashed. Some of the color returned to her face. She opened her eyes.

I noticed the water level in the tide pool had gone down to just below Kalea's nipples.

The tide ebbed quickly. The crowd moved as if to pull her from the pit, but Rowena stopped them.

"She must stay in until the pool is empty," she said grimly. As she spoke, the clouds broke. The sun shone, bright and warm. Kalea had lived, but as far as I could see she looked if she were hanging on to life by a thread.

Time passed in long, silent moments. Finally, Rowena said, "The pool is empty. Pull her out."

I helped extract her. Her body felt like ice. She barely breathed. We laid her out on a warm shelf of rock in the sun. Her chest rose and fell feebly.

Brenna gazed at her a long time, and then, to my astonishment (and everyone else's), pulled her dress over her head, lay down beside Kalea, and wound her arms and legs around her pressing her their bodies together. After a moment of stunned silence, another woman walked forward, stripped, and embraced Kalea on the other side. Brenna my wife and the other woman sandwiched her, imparting their warmth. Some women ran off to their houses and came back carrying quilts. Color returned to Kalea's face and lips. After maybe twenty minutes, two women replaced Brenna and the other. I helped her put her garment back on.

The village women kept Kalea warm in shifts. After a time, when she had recovered enough to speak, Rowena ordered Jannet to give her strong drink and some food. Six men took up the quilts and carried her in them back to the temple.

The next day I received a summons from Rowena. She offered me wine.

"Where did you get this?" I asked.

"In Vorthr's home. It seems he developed a taste for it in his negotiation with the Romans. He had three smalls casks of it buried in his floor."

"Kalea?"

"She is well. We will be speaking with her in a short while."

"Why did you save her from hanging?"

"She knows something she is not telling us."

"You think so?"

"I can read it in her eyes. She is a good woman—kind, generous, full of love and virtue. Such souls find it hard to be deceitful. She is holding something back. She will tell us now."

"You said the goddess spoke to you."

"She did—in the way we discussed not long ago. Yes, my perception brought on my intervention. No, I did not hear a voice. Yet I was impelled to this action and Freya had a part in it."

I paused and then asked, "You said you survived the tide pool?"

"When I came here, I thought I would simply begin to function as a priestess in Freya's temple. I arrived, the priestess and the leaders took me down to the shore, stripped me naked as the day I was born in front of the whole village, tied me up, and put me up to my neck in freezing water. I managed to survive. I didn't want to die and fought with everything in me to live. I passed out and woke up three days later in a bed in the temple compound. Kalea did much better than I did. Of course, she had encouragement from your wife and the other women in the village—more than what I had in my hour of trial."

Jannet entered the room, bowed, and said Kalea was ready.

She looked weary and haggard. The girls had braided her hair and dressed her in a simple white garment. She bowed to the ground. Rowena told her to rise up and to sit.

She sat, folding her strong hands, interlocking her long fingers. She did not look at Rowena or at me. Rowena reached over and gently touched her hands.

"I am sorry for your loss, child."

"Thank you, Lady Priestess."

"I am not a married woman and cannot know the depth of your sorrow, but I give you my heart and my love."

Kalea did not answer. Tears filled her eyes splashed down her cheeks.

"You know something you have not told us, Kalea," she continued. "It is something vital; something we must know. The goddess spared your life. She will give your life back to you once you reveal what this thing is. And reveal it you will."

Kalea looked up. Her hollow, weary eyes met Rowena's gaze.

"Give me up the truth, my daughter."

"The village of Ciobre is planning treachery against this place and its people. They are meeting with the Romans when the full moon wanes. They plan to lead the Roman soldiers through the wood and fall upon us."

Silence came. Kalea looked down at her hands.

"Why did you conceal this?"

"My brother lives in Ciobre." Silence came again. "I did not want to see him and his family die. I will take my own life to atone for my sin in not revealing their treachery," she said.

"The goddess spared you. That is your reason to live. You will remain here as a temple servant for three years. Your children are with other families now, but you will be permitted to see them and, at the end of your time here, they will be returned to you and the temple will support you until you remarry, if you chose to do so. You had no choice but to obey your husband. The people know that your hurt is deep. It may be healed."

"You are kind, my Lady."

"Give praise to the Goddess. It is her will that you live. Do not disobey her by undoing your own life or you will face eternal torment."

"I will obey her."

Rowena called Jannet, who took Kalea out of the room. Rowena looked over at me.

"So we are in danger of attack."

"Apparently. You were right about Kalea. I admire your mercy toward her."

"She is a guileless, holy woman. We need more of her type."

"What do we do?"

"We attack and destroy Ciobre."

"Do you think that would be the best course of action?"

"I thought it was the only course of action open to us."

"I have an idea," I said.

~~~

V

We moved through the morning fog. The silent forest dripped with moisture. Thin, grey rays of dawn filtered through the canopy of leaves and branches, casting faint light. By now my legs and boots were soaked with dew. I followed the men of the village, who knew their way without the illumination of the sun. I carried two swords and had worn my Atlantian robe, more for warmth than anything else. I went grimly, remembering the sea fights I had been in — the confusion, blood, death, screams, curses, came into my mind to revolt me with memories of loss and destruction. I thought of the attack by the Azteca. A shudder I could not disguise passed over my body. The trees thinned. We came to the village and stopped at the edge of the clearing.

Silence hovered over the rows of thatched-roof houses. Smoke rose straight up from the chimneys. A few people were up. Two women bore water from the spring. They smiled and chattered as they walked together. A man gathered sticks for his fireplace.

I surveyed the village through the mist, my eyes rested on a sight that made me instantly tense and alert. Beside of the larger houses I spotted a Roman staff pushed into the ground, the gold eagle and the letters SPQR. Around it stood banners and symbolic icons. I got Gavin's attention. He came close, leaning into me. I pointed and mouthed "Romans." Gavin gazed and nodded. He summoned four of the best fighters in the village, who fell in rank behind him. All of us tensed as the light increased. Gavin raised his sword. We stood poised. I sensed everyone holding his breath. Gavin lowered his blade. The army roared a battle cry and rushed into the village. My squad ran toward the house with the Roman banners.

In only a moment the army of Freyathorp and the other villages in the clan engulfed Ciobre like a tidal wave. The fighters seized anyone walking through the common, began to enter houses and rousted the inhabitants out. Gavin and Rowena had wanted to destroy the village and massacre its inhabitants, but I pointed out that the treachery lay with the leadership and the innocent should not die, and my counsel prevailed.

The group of warriors I was with broke through the door, swords and axes in hand. Three village men and four Romans sat around a table. Cups of beer, bread and cheese sat before them. They rose quickly and reached for their weapons (they had stacked them in a corner). Our select warriors interposed. The Romans and the leaders of Ciobe put their hands in the air in a gesture of surrender. More warriors joined us. In only a moment, the main room had filled with armed men

I noticed one of the Romans was a Proconsul. A unit commander and two officers stood near him.

Outnumbered and hemmed in, they had the sense not to try to fight us. And Proconsuls are most often not skillful soldiers but political appointees. The three village leaders—all older men—looked fearful. I came forward and spoke gesturing.

"*Operor non reluctor,*" I said. "*Vos mos non exsisto vulnero si vos trado volutarie.*"[4]

"*Nos mos non reluctor,*"[5] the Procounsul said.

I spoke to Gavin. "Let us keep the Romans as separate prisoners. What do you plan to do to the village leaders?"

"We will take them to the Lady Priestess for judgment."

This surprised me. Gavin led in military matters and no one in the village disputed his authority. It seemed strange he would submit his prisoners to Rowena.

We separated the Romans from the villager leaders. Heavily armed groups of warriors escorted them back to Freyathorpe. By now the citizens of the settlement had assembled on the village common. They gasped with astonishment as the Roman soldiers and their own leaders marched them into captivity. Soon more armed men from the other three villages in the tribe arrived. The people of Ciobre, unarmed and assembled, looked fearful. Gavin addressed them,

---

[4] Do not resist. You will not be harmed if you surrender willingly.
[5] We will not resist.

assuring them they would not be harmed. He explained what had happened. I followed the entourage guarding the Roman prisoners back to Freythorpe.

We took the roads this time. The sun had cleared the horizon. Birds sang. The fog dissolved. I let myself relax. It had been a bloodless capture. I wondered what would happen next, though I felt better about the situation knowing Rowena, not Gavin, had command of it.

We arrived. Still another large force from the other villages in the tribe had arrived, armed and angry. They brandished their weapons and ground their teeth when they saw the Romans and the traitorous leaders of Ciobe. The sound of some four-hundred men grinding their teeth unnerved me. Gavin cleared a path. The tribesmen shook their fists and shouted as the prisoners made their way to the Temple of Freya.

Rowena awaited them. She stood tall and terrible in the authority of her position. Onela and Jannet stood on either side of her. Jannet held a small image of Freya. Like the larger image of Freya in the sanctuary, Onela held a holy spring and a bowl of sacrificial blood. Rowena looked terrible and stern. The crowd of villager fell quiet. Gavin pushed the three leaders forward. Rowena regarded them a few moments and then spoke.

"Death."

Gavin and his soldiers pushed the men to their knees. They did not resist. They had committed treason. Their clansmen had uncovered it. They would die and they deserved to die. Three of Gavin's lieutenants unsheathed swords and decapitated the trio. Their heads flew through the air, their bodies fell to the ground. Blood spurted form the stumps of their necks. The people did not cheer. The three executioners picked up the heads, jammed them on points of spears, and pushed the butts of the spears into the ground

I heard a new commotion. Soldiers came, pulling three struggling, wailing women before them. The men shoved them to the ground in front of Rowena. They lifted their hands, wept, and begged.

"Death," Rowena said.

The women screamed. One vomited. The men seized them and dragged them back to the tree line to hang them.

When the wailing and pleading of the women faded, Rowena spoke to the assembly.

"The goddess has revealed this to us. We will sacrifice a heifer to her this night. There is to be no retribution against the people of Ciobe. We will enact a studied judgment. If others in the village are guilty, they will pay the price. But the village shall not be destroyed. As for our Roman captives, we will question them and decide upon a course of action. Those of you who have not been chosen as scouts to search for enemy forces, return to your homes. Be ready to fight in a moment. Be vigilant. Our villages will not be overcome."

The people cheered at this. The men raised their weapons and shouted as the women screamed a war cry. After a time, they quieted down and dispersed.

A group of young men appeared and carried off the decapitated corpses, leaving the heads on spears. I let my gaze wander to the tree line where the bodies of the three women dangled from ropes. One was still alive, her feet kicking weakly. A group of women stood watching her. I walked over to Rowena.

"Did the women have to die?"

"They would have eventually stirred up the urge for revenge. They had to be silenced."

"Where are the Romans?"

"In a cow barn that belongs to the temple."

"We need to talk to them. Have them brought to the temple. We don't want to question them in a cow barn. I invited Gavin."

Rowena told Kalea to bring bread and beer. I stole glances at her as she went about her business, wondered if she chaffed against the bit and bridle that so firmly held her in place and outlined the perimeters of her life in such a restrictive fashion. First she had been a temple maiden of Vesta and then a woman dedicated to the goddess Freya. She had lost her virginity not in response to love but in response to prophecy. Or had she? What if she had simply rebelled against the strictures that had held her as a votary for so long? What then? I thought about Brenna.

Kalea appeared. She wore a white dress like Jannet and Olena—the garment of one who had received manumission to the goddess. Her hair was braided behind (not on the side, which was a marker indicating virginity). Kalea was an uncommonly beautiful woman. I recalled seeing her naked body when she put in the tide pool. She set out the bread and a beer and then came a bowed to Rowena.

"Are the prisoners here?"

"Yes, my lady. They are guarded and wait outside the door. Gavin and the leaders of the village also approach."

"Thank you, Kalea. Arise and attend me."

Kalea took her place at Rowena's side. I heard doors open and the clomp of feet. Some of the younger top warriors of the clan came in, the two ranking Romans following them.

The Romans looked weary and disheveled. The Commander showed only a slight flicker of fear in his eyes. The Procounsul seemed more anxious and uncomprehending. They came before Rowena and me. Soon Gavin took up position behind us.

"We have brought you here to question you," Rowena said in Latin. "I am Rowena, Priestess of the Goddess Freya. Here is Gavin, leader of our village; and Aschel, a citizen of our village who is a warrior and knows your language. Speak the truth and it will go better for you. Tell me your names."

The Romans glanced at each other. The

Commander spoke first.

"I am Flavius Marcus Quintus of the Gemina Legion. This is" —

"He has a tongue," Rowena interrupted. "He can speak for himself."

"I am Horatius Egnatius Gallienus, Proconsul of Legion Valeria Victrix."

"The Valeria Victrix is quartered in Exeter, I believe."

They hesitated and then saw it would be pointless to lie or obfuscate.

"It is."

"What has brought you all this way?"

They balked at answering this.

"Speak. We know the truth," I said. "You met with the leaders of Ciobe in order to subordinate that village. You were seeking allies. The only reason you would do this is in preparation to invade our territory."

They knew they were cornered. Gavin and the guards could not understand the conversation but could read the nuances of the men's looks and stances. The Romans had dealt with Celts before. They knew Gavin the others wanted to kill them.

"Our commanders are interested in acquiring this territory and bringing it into union with the lands we already control here in Albion."

Rowena translated this for Gavin and the others. Their eyes grew wild and they bristled with rage. Rowena noticed the Romans' uneasiness.

"No one will harm you, as you are in the sacred precincts of the Temple. Thank the goddess Freya for her protection. Otherwise you would be hewn to pieces. Do your superiors want our tin mines? Is that what motivates your desire to seize this province?"

"Perhaps."

"Is violence necessary? Access to our mines could be obtained through negotiation."

They did not reply.

"Tonight you will dine with us. My women will clean your clothes and allow you to bathe. This audience is at an end."

Rowena told Gavin the others he wished to speak further with the Romans. Gavin nodded. I could see the desire for murder in his eyes. Rowena noticed it too.

"Be certain our prisoners are not harmed," she told him. "No profit will come from killing them."

Gavin nodded. The guards took the Romans away. Rowena turned to Kalea.

"Leave us," she said. Kalea bowed and left. Rowena watched her go out the door. "We need to bring this to an end," she said. "Gavin and the others will not tolerate the presence of the Romans for too much longer."

I nodded, thinking over courses of action we might take. Rowena's hands on my arm started me. I looked over at her. She leaned in and kissed me.

Rowena and I had been lovers, but I knew the time of "unleashing" the power of Freya had passed. In fact, the village had attended a ceremony to thank the goddess for intervening and recognizing Rowena's role as the vessel for the unleashing. Though I am not certain when the ceremony articulated it, I got the impression that things would go back to where they had been before. Rowena would return to her role as the priestess, holy to Freya (even if she were not a virgin anymore). I would assume to my status as a married villager. Brenna told me that most of the priestesses who gave themselves as vessels eventually married, though they continued in their service to the deity.

I resisted at first, but her kisses, her arms around me, pulled out a truth I knew and had denied. I loved her as much as she loved me. Her office of priestess stood as a barrier to any relationship we might have. My marriage and my love and sense of loyalty to Brenna inhibited me from expressing my desire for her. All of that melted away and she hungrily kissed me and as I responded. I ran my hands over her body, squeezing her breasts and her hips. She ran over and locked the door. We could not lie on the stone floor so I made love to her squatting. The Mayans preferred this method and several Mayan prostitutes I had paid for in the old days in Chasca had taught me the technique. She seemed to know it as well.

We embraced until we both were spent.

She collapsed into my arms. We held each other. Silence was the proper response.

"No one must know of this," she whispered after a while.

I nodded.

"It will be difficult to conceal, but I could not hold back the flood of what I feel for you, Aschel. I love you. I've loved you from the moment I laid eyes on you. I knew you were an Atlantian by your dress and knew your ways would be the ways of your people, who are wise and strong. We are in danger. As priestess my only choice is to marry or to live without men. Now that you have opened the door to passion and desire, there is no closing it. My love for you is wrong in every way and will bring the wrath of Freya upon us, but I love you."

I lightly kissed her lips.

"If Freya is the goddess of love and of the passion that goes with it, I don't see how she could be displeased with what we've done."

She did not reply. After a while, we cleaned up as best we could. Rowena called in Jannet and sent me on my way.

VI

The day after Rowena and I began our liaison, Brenna announced she was pregnant again.

"I will bear you another son," she beamed.

"I think it would be charming to have a daughter."

She looked puzzled.

'"You don't desire a son?"

"I have a son. He's strong and healthy. A girl child is sweet, gentle, and beloved of her father. If she is as kind and sweet as you, I'll feel like I've come to the land of blessed souls."

Tears came to her eyes. The kind and tender things I said to her often pierced her heat—I think because she so seldom heard endearments such as I spoke. I wiped her tears and kissed her.

Things were tense in the village. Many thought the Romans would attack. Our scouts located their main encampment, ten miles past the most outlying village in the tribe. They reckoned the numbers at around a thousand. Rowena, who knew the formations of the Roman Army, said it was probably a First Cohort, a double-strength cohort that, since that division of the Roman army numbered around a thousand. The scouts also reported that just as many auxiliary troops recruited from the British tribes were with them. Our villages could muster probably five-hundred men. Though brave and skillful, they were no match or the Romans with their tactics and superior weaponry; add their force of British axillaries, and the situation was not in our favor.

We had the Roman officers as hostages, but Rowena warned the council not to count on this as a deterrent.

"They will not withdraw merely to save

two officers and some lower-ranking men. If they want this land badly, the will still attack."

I was afraid of an attack by sea. It would be easy for the Romans to bring ships to the bay and effect a landing. Perhaps they planned to hit by land and sea, crushing the tribe between two columns. When I told Rowena this she said it was likely.

At night I lay in bed with Brenna. Our child grew in her womb. Balder slept in his crib. I thought of him enslaved. I thought of Brenna torn from my arms, raped and abused, and then carried off to a life of bondage. I thought of the people of the village—brave, good, and strong— massacred and enslaved. The warmth of Brenna's body, the quiet intimacy I had come to know with her, made everything in me that could respond cry against what Fate had brought to bear upon us. There had to be a way to stop it.

As the week sped by, I slept with Rowena twice more. I could not control my passion when she summoned me. Guilt over my betrayal of Brenna flooded my soul.

And there was more. Talking about having a girl made me think of Lark and Trella. I remembered them, their innocence and beauty, the strong but fragile life of children. Their death had been a crime—and whatever forces or deities, if any at all, brought about their end, I had learned from their loss that evil can prevail over good. Evil prevails most of the time. My children and wife had been taken from me by a natural catastrophe. Now I faced the same prospect from military invasion.

Brenna stirred. My guilt surged when I thought of her simple, unaffected love. Once I had told Rowena that Brenna was a child. I had been wrong in my assessment of her. The wisdom of goodness lay deep in her soul. I, not she, had received the greater blessing in the marriage neither of us had asked for.

The next day the village was abuzz with news. Our scouts had seen a formation of Roman ships lying off a chain of islands ten miles out to sea. The Roman camp looked like it was preparing to march. I had been correct. The Romans planned to catch us in a vice grip. They had the resources and the numbers to do it.

Gavin wanted to kill our prisoners and send their heads to the Roman commanders. He grew more impatient with Rowena. Both she and I realized that a discovery of our liaison would be the excuse he needed to kill us. With Rowena out of the way, he could lead his people in a headlong berserker attack. They would die in a blaze of glory. Slavery and abjection would follow. There seemed no way now to escape from this.

Olena came to tell me Rowena wished to speak with me. Brenna had taken Balder to the house of a friend. I was glad she was not present to hear Olena's message — though, of course, she would hear of it soon enough. Everyone knew everything what went on in the village. If Rowena and I had kept our relationship a secret, we would not keep it a secret for much longer. I walked through the village to the temple. People were out, tending gardens and making repairs on their houses. Women hung out wash. A teenage girl slopped hogs. Herds of boisterous children romped and shouted. And men honed their swords or the upcoming battle.

I entered the Temple. Kalea led me to the sanctuary where Rowena sat on her heels before the image of Freya. I came up beside her. I took her hand.

"I know what I must do," she said.

I did not ask what. I waited for her to speak again.

"I never thought I would know a man," she said. "I thought I would live and die a virgin and had resigned myself to that. Now I have known your love. I never thought I would know death — though that's silly, since we all die."

I felt a tug at my heart and in my throat.

"You don't mean you're going to kill yourself."

"No. That would be the noble thing to do. My Roman father would approve. But I'm too much of a coward to do it. And remember, I am a dedicated woman. My life is not my own."

I glanced at the image of Freya.

"The goddess has spoken to me." A trace of irony rang in her voice, though she still sounded grim. "It does not matter whether it arose from my mind or my heart or whether is a direct revelation. It does not matter if I heard it from Aasgard or my own imagination. The goddess controls all things. My heart is her possession. She has spoken to me." She looked up at me. "I've done foolish things, Aschel. But who can stop love? The goddess will bring it to an end."

I waited for a long time for her to speak. Finally, I said, "Is it a foolish thing to fall in love?"

"It is for me."

"Doesn't the goddess know you're human?"

"She knows my heart. That is my only comfort."

I thought she might want to embrace one last time, but she sent me away after telling me she had called an assembly for tomorrow morning. She did not say more. When I returned home, Brenna told me the news I already knew. An assembly would convene after breakfast. She added, "We're going to war."

It was true. At the assembly, Rowena looked grave. Her voice, subdued, the crowd silent to hear her, the noise of birds and waves lapping the shoreline in the background, she said the goddess had spoken to her. She had ordered the village to war.

"Remember how faithful the goddess has been to us. She revealed the treachery of Vorthr and of the elders from Ciobre. We should not fear the call to war. The Romans are even now advancing on us. We are hemmed in by an army on one side and by warships on the other. We will intercept and strike them before they can crush us between the stones of their aggression."

Normally, the people would have sent up a war cry and a cheer, but Rowena's demeanor — she stood flanked by Jannet and Olena; Kalea stood behind them — so solemn and dignified, exuding the power of holiness and of her goddess — stilled their voice

"I will march in front of our armies. I will bear the image of Freya against them. It is she, my children, who has enabled us to prevail so far. I cast myself upon her care. It may be she will make me a sacrifice. I am pledged already and my life is not my own. I die willing if this is the path she chooses for me. Whatever happens, we will come to fight them in power and holiness. Assemble yourselves. We go out this very day."

Gavin had already sent word to the other villages. The men made love to their wives, kissed their children, armed themselves, and assembled to march toward the rendezvous point. Jannet and Onela visited their families for what very likely would be the last time. Weeping and resolve filled Freyathorp. Brenna cried in bed. I kissed her good-bye and embraced my son, who was bewildered and upset by his mother's tears. I slung on my swords and joined the quiet, solemn line of men marching out to face the Roman army.

Our scouts led us to a wood near a wide,

rocky meadow. The ranks of fighters swelled as the men of the other villages joined. Many had painted their faces blue and dyed their hair red. The weapons, war paint, the grim, determined countenances, made our force look frightening. But we were up against a war machine that had conquered all the land around the Mediterranean Sea and most of Europa. Tribal bravado could not defeat calculated military technique. We were outnumbered. Our weapons were inferior. We did not have the element of surprise. The Roman forward parties had seen us.

They formed ranks at the edge of the thick wood that bounded the meadow on either side. The red-cloaked legionaries occupied the center. Their British auxiliaries assembled on their flanks like appendages, like the horns on the head of a red bull. Their standards shone in the sun. Their banners fluttered in the summer wind. Their weapons and armor glittered in the sun.

We came out of the tree line and formed lines. When all our warriors were in place, they parted in the center.

Rowena, splendid and beautiful, dressed in a scarlet robe embroidered with gold, her hair braided, the small image of Freya in her arms, stepped forward. Olena and Jannet, in their white acolyte dresses, their hair untied, one carrying a holly bob, one a bowl of sacrificial blood, stood on either side of her. Kalea, also in white, stood behind them.

Everyone in the army seemed to hold his

breath. Rowena stood a moment and then started walking forward at a slow, regular pace. We followed her.

A hundred yards of ground separated us. I realized this day would most probably mean my death. As we approached I heard the noise of the Roman and British troops readying their weapons. Swords and javelins scraped, leather armor creaked, the sound of bows being drawn, came to my ears. I knew the Romans began their battles with a fusillade of arrows and javelins. Then they charged. They would cut us down like a farmer scythed wheat.

As we drew closer, though, the commander of the Roman forces told his men to stand down. They eased down their bows and put their javelins at present arms. We advanced. Tension rose like an invisible dome, enveloping both sides. About fifteen feet from where the Roman commander stood, Rowena stopped. Jannet and Olena put the objects they had carried on the ground on either side of her and turned, solemn faced, toward us. We knew by the look on their faces that they were ordering us to go no further and take no hostile action against the Romans.

We were close enough to see Romans in their full military glory. They looked impressive in their red uniforms. Many were sturdy Roman stock, Italian, like the Romans I had met in my diplomatic missions. But I saw black men, blond Germans, many who looked like the villagers (but were legionaries, not auxiliary troops). They looked tense but resigned. The wind blew. Silence deepened. The Roman commander called a tribal man to his side.

"Ask her," he began.

"I speak your language," Rowena interrupted.

He nodded surprised that she spoke Latin and spoke it so well.

"I am Rowena, Priestess of the Goddess Freya. I come, and my army comes, in her power."

The commander gazed at our force. Reading his expression, I could see he knew his side would win but also knew it would be a costly fight.

"We don't want violence," he said.

"If you don't want violence, why have you come to our land with an army? And why have you moored warships near my village?"

He smiled blandly. "We only come to free our officers and centurions, whom you have captured."

"They are here with us."

When she did not elaborate, he asked, "Are you willing to return them to us—to negotiate an exchange?"

"What do you have to exchange?" she asked.

He smiled at her shrewdness.

"We can arrange a withdrawal."

"A withdrawal is easily reversed."

"True."

"Is there some reason your officers plotted with the elders of Ciobe?"

"We are interested in mining."

"Establishing mines does not necessitate enslaving a people, does it?"

"No one meant to enslave you."

"I would like to believe this. I would like to believe you are as benevolent as you seem to be. Our encounters with you so far have suggested otherwise."

He looked around.

"If you wish to negotiate with us, our present disposition," he made a circular gesture with his arm, "is probably not the best arrangement."

"I agree."

"I will send my army back to our base camp. I will signal our ships to return to port. Will you disband your force as well?"

"We will not attack you if you agree to leave. In two days, come to my village by ship—one ship, no more than four *contubernium*. You have my word as Priestess of Freya that no harm will come to you. We will return two of your companions today as earnest of the others and so you may know that they are well and unharmed. I bring them before you now."

She nodded to Kalea, who hurried to the wood and emerged with our four prisoners. They walked over to join the Roman commander. They looked well, though afraid to be in the center of a potential melee. They clasped the Roman commander's hand and embraced him and other friends. Rowena freed one of the officers and one of the centurions and returned the others to the woods and captivity. After that, she called Olean and Jannet and told them to kneel on either side of her. I think she did this knowing the long march, the tension, and standing so long might cause one of them faint. They knelt, white-faced, probably convinced they would die and possibly be raped. Duty strengthened their resolve. It shone through their fear.

I felt our army tense. We had come to a decisive point. The Roman commander might break his word, order an attack, and proceed with the plan to annex our territory to the Province of Albion. I had no idea if he would keep his word. I was also afraid the fear and tension our men felt might lead to a spontaneous charge. I think the Roman commander realized the same.

"I agree to your terms. I will withdraw our forces. I will tell our flotilla to sail home. In two days we will come to your village—one ship, thirty-two soldiers. No treachery."

Rowena nodded. The Roman commander signaled. His drummer struck up a tocsin. Trumpets blared. The army did a left face and, banners flying, standards held high, marched away from the place where there had almost been a battle.

We returned to the camp. A wail of joy went up from the women. Brenna came running, leaping high in the air, and fell in my arms, almost knocking me over. She kissed and kissed me. Balder scurried over. I picked him up as he laughed and kicked.

When Rowena returned, the women and the men too old to fight prostrated themselves before her. One of our warriors carried Jannet, who had passed out from fear and stress. Olena sobbed as she walked. Kalea comforted her. Rowena looked exhausted. As she walked on, many women got up and ran to her to kiss her face or to touch the hem of her robe. She retired to the temple, taking her acolytes with her.

Rejoicing filled the space of our village, though some said we should not be so elated because the Romans still might betray us. Our scouts reported the next day that the Romans had marched back to their base camp. Their ships had furled sail and headed east. Gavin sent the men from the other village back, though he instructed them to be ready to assemble at a moment's notice.

Brenna told me the women of the village were certain we would all be killed by the Romans and they would be enslaved. She had sharpened a knife to kill Balder and readied a rope to hang herself if the Romans or their allies had appeared in the village. She considered what Rowena had done as miraculous. Many said she was not a priestess but the Goddess Freya herself come in human form to be the savior of the tribe.

I did not see Rowena that first day. The

trauma of walking into what seemed certain death had no doubt harrowed her as much as it had Jannet and Olena. I wondered how she regarded her new status as an avatar.

The Romans sent word that Claudius Flavius Aëtius, the commander, would arrive by ship on the morning of the next day. I received a summons from Rowena the night before his scheduled arrival.

I had wondered if she would call for me. I did not think it would be wise. If I left, Brenna would know why and where I had gone. The villagers were on edge and tense and might be up and notice movement in the camp or activity at the Temple. And Rowena seemed to have come to a new plateau of religious commitment. I rested next to Brenna until a hand touched my shoulder in the middle of the night.

I started awake. In the moonlight filtering through the open door, I saw Kalea. She put her finger to her lips, pointed with her other hand, and slipped out, leaving the door open..

Beyond the threshold, the full moon bathed the village in white light. Its reflection, like a long path leading to the stars, divided the waters of the bay. The stars blazed. Owls hooted in the trees. I pulled on a pair of trousers and went outside.

Kalea, in her acolyte dress, waited a few feet from the front door of my house. She turned and moved toward the trees. He white garment made her look like a spirit or a ghost. I followed her into the forest. She led me to where Rowena stood.

I gazed at Rowena. She wore her purple cloak. Kalea stepped back, fading like an apparition into the dark.

"I have to see you this last time," she said.

"Last time?"

"I feel it will be our last time together, yes. I don't want to explain. We have only an hour before the village stirs."

She unhooked her cloak and dropped it.

She stood there, moonlight drenching her naked, beautiful body. Rowena was tall and had a strong, lithe form. As a girl, she told me once, she had trained and worked on her strength and posture. Her superior in the order of vestals had the idea that a vestal should be trim and fit, not shapeless and overweight. Her long, muscular legs supported her firm hips, the curve of her pubis, and her flat stomach. Her breasts, high above the well-developed ribcage, hung like ripe melons. Her shoulders were strong, her posture straight.

"Make love to me this last time," she said.

I removed my trousers. The summer night was warm and still. I did not want to kneel this time, so I lifted her, lowering her on to my member. She wrapped her legs around my hips and we began to move.

Most of the time our lovemaking was ferocious, wild, and violent, especially when I got on top of her, or she on top of me, in bed. This time, however (and because of the restrictions of the position we had chosen), it was slow, tender, and intimate. I thrust gently as she moaned and gasped, her legs thighs around me, breasts rubbing against my chest, her long hair shining in the silvery light Diana shed (or Rhiannon, as the people of the village called the moon goddess). I kissed her. She whispered tender words to me, bit my ears and touched them with her tongue. She stiffened as her orgasm came, tilting her head back (almost tipping us over), a quiet scream from her throat echoing through the moonlit wood. Then she put her cheek against my shoulder, tightening the enclosing circle of her womanhood so I came quickly after that.

She unlocked her legs, pulled herself up and then down and off me.

"No words. I will go."

Kalea appeared with Rowena's cloak. She threw it over her mistress and the two of them disappeared into the darkened trees.

I threw my pants on and hurried back to the village. Years of being at sea taught me when the dawn would come. I had lived here long enough to develop sensitivity to the rhythms of nature in the forest shoreline. I knew the predawn noises that often woke Balder. They had started. I stole back to the house and climbed in bed with Brenna. She instinctively snuggled against me but did not wake. I slept maybe two hours. When Brenna awoke, she insisted we make love. Luckily, enough time had passed from when I was with Rowena that I could do something for her. By the time I left her and our child, the sun had appeared as a thin shell of light over the bay.

Nostalgia for the sea often overwhelms me. As I stood on the shore and looked out at the breakers under the vast expanse of sky, and saw waves lapping the beach, I felt a longing to sail. I had spent my life on the water. My father took me out on the water just after I learned to walk. I was sailing solo by the time I was ten years old and had my own boat when I was thirteen. Being a landlubber frustrated me at times. My boat, stored in a shed I had built for it, languished on logs, its hull probably rotting by now, just like its tattered sails.

As I looked out to sea, a vessel came around the edge of the bay. No wind blew, so the crew rowed it. I anxiously looked for other ships, wondering if they would keep their word. No other vessel followed. A crowd of our men gathered on the shore, Gavin leading them. Gavin had a new respect for Rowena now and had given in to the idea that he should take his orders from her. The vessel drew to shore. The Romans threw out ropes. Crewmen leaped in the water to pull the vessel in. The men of my village lent a hand.

They let down a gangplank and Claudius disembarked. He wore his dress uniform—longer tunic and more draping, gold trim and an ornamented helmet. His troop marched down behind him, single file, and formed ranks once they were on shore, their red uniforms bright in the morning sunlight. I noticed archers stood ready on the ship. They had mounted two ballista on the deck, aimed, no doubt, at Gavin and Rowena. Still, I understood this as a precaution against treachery from us and not as treachery on their part.

The Romans looked good. A glance showed me the grudging admiration on the faces of Gavin and the armed men he had picked as his guard. Military men admired others who know how to fight. The unstated mutual admiration would help. Beside Claudius, a lieutenant carried a banner of the legion. Claudius came to a halt. He bowed to Rowena.

"I greet you in the name of the Senate and People of Rome."

"And we return your greeting in the name of the Goddess Freya. Let us go to her Temple and speak. Our soldiers will wait outside. You may put your men at ease."

Claudius turned and told his men to break rank. They relaxed, assuming a looser formation. Gavin's men relaxed as well. Six of us—Rowena, Claudius, Gavin, Kalea, the young Roman lieutenant, and I—went into the Temple to negotiate.

As I walked near Rowena, I thought of last night. I thought of holding her in my arms, the beauty of her bare form in the warmth and moonlight. I thought of the tender fury of our lovemaking. Somehow I agreed with her. Last night marked the finality of our relationship. I would never make love to her again. I would never know intimacy with her. We would not even share a good-bye. I don't believe in gods or goddesses, yet Fate seemed to exist as a controlling force in the universe. Fate directed our lives. The ponderous workings of Fate had aligned themselves, and a by-product of the alignment would be our separation. We came inside the Temple of Freya.

Rowena made a short obeisance to the image of the goddess. We went to the reception hall and sat down at a long wooden table.

The Roman commander took off his helmet. He smiled (slyly, I thought), and then spoke.

"I thought it odd," he said, "to encounter a woman who speaks Latin like a native and has the gestures and carriage of a highborn Roman lady. It stirred my memory. I had heard of a Roman girl—I believe she was a Vestal, a hostage raised in Londinium and then in Rome, who opted to leave and return to her own people. I believe I have found just such a woman—Priestess Rowena—Drusilla, daughter of Horatius Germanicus Glacialis. I believe you have gone by both Rowena and Drusilla in your variegated life."

She curled her lip just slightly—something between a smile and a sneer.

"Well done, Captain. Your investigative skills are impressive."

"You overestimate my abilities. You have

become something of a legend in our part of this island. People speak of the Roman Queen who rules a vast, powerful realm in the wilds of the east and is beautiful beyond description."

"You should see that this legend, like most legends, is false."

"I would say that last part about your being beautiful is entirely accurate."

"I am no queen. The realm I preside over as priestess consists of five villages and perhaps four-thousand people. We are neither wealthy nor powerful."

"I can see that—though a great deal of wealth rests in the bowels of the earth under our feet."

All this time I had been translating for Gavin. I left out that Claudius knew of her Roman past and made up small talk, adding that this was customary among Romans when they began negotiations. I began translating truthfully with the remark Claudius made about wanting to mine tin.

"The ore is valuable," he went on. "It can be smelted, supplying our needs for metal here in the Province of Albion. We might even sell it for profit elsewhere in the empire. The work, plus an addition of people to this region, would bring prosperity."

"And the imposition of Roman rule would bring the loss of our freedom as a people."

"The region need not be annexed. It could exist as an autonomous area under Roman protection. We don't want a revolt on our hands. Your rule five villages. Yet there are thousands of your people from other tribes and clans in the area. If we move against you, it would mean a general revolt. I don't want that, neither does the army or the civilian administration."

"You suborned a village."

"We did so on the orders of a politician with connections to Rome that made everyone afraid to contradict him. They bring these young fellows up here to give them experience at governance and they end up causing endless headaches for us. Fortunately, this particular young scion got in a quarrel with his companion, which led to a knife fight, and—well, may the gods rest his soul in Elysium. We only brought an army into your territory to rescue Flavius and Horatius, who are good men and worth their salt as commanders. We don't want war."

"How can we be certain this is true?"

"Do you remember Atticus Aurelian Zeyphrinius?"

Usually a paragon of calm, Rowena flinched.

"Of course I remember him."

"His broken heart has never mended. Even volunteering to serve in this, our northernmost province, has not assuaged his grief."

"He is here?"

"Indeed. He sends his greetings. My proposal is as follows. Marry Atticus. He will settle here with you. We will establish a colony city for miners a little distance from here. Atticus will serve as commander of the garrison. Your people are welcome to live there and to work in the mines—or to live here and work in the mines. As a matter of fact, we would value the expertise in mining your people possess. They have the reputation of being skillful in that area. I know we could learn from them."

Rowena still was nonplussed.

"I will have to consider this," she finally said. "And, of course, it will require the approval of Gavin and the Counsel."

"Of course. Atticus is here. I took the liberty of inviting him along. He's on the ship. It's cramped below-decks and I'm sure he would be happy to come up in the sunlight. I can bring him here if you wish to see him."

I translated. Gavin gaped. Rowena was so astonished and shaken that she could hardly speak or maintain her diplomatic and priestly bearing. She did not reply.

"Of course," Claudius said, "if you would deem it inappropriate . . ."

My mind flashed to one of the times Rowena and I had lain together in a pile of thick quilts, our bodies hot, our spirits sated with love.

"I never thought I would do anything like this," she had said then. "I had been pledged twice: once as a vestal, once as Priestess of Freya. As Priestess of Freya, I might be allowed to marry, but many of her priestesses never did because the men in the village are afraid of a representative of the goddess. The last three priestesses before me had never married—and, of course, a priestess has to set an example for the young girls who look up her. In Rome, I didn't have the option to marry—well, I did, but not until I was thirty-six, after I had done thirty years of service to the Convent of Vesta. By then you're too old to have children and the same thing happens as happens here. The men don't want to marry because you were a vestal—a sacred, holy girl. Even though you can to marry after you leave the service of the temple, hardly any of the vestals do. I'd put aside the idea of ever lying with a man."

"Were you ever in love?"

She took a moment to answer.

"Once. I hesitate to speak of it because it was so powerful. It happened when we were in Atlantis."

"You don't have to talk about it."

"I want to tell you, Aschel. It will do my soul good to share the story with someone. You're the only person I'm able to share it with."

She paused, licked her lips, and went on.

"Vestals live apart from men, of course. I served in the Temple but I stayed home with my family. Vestals are trusted. Confidential material—wills, deeds, money—is kept in the Temple of Vesta because the priestesses cannot be bribed or suborned. That's why Daddy took me along on diplomatic trips. I would carry the documents, treaties, letters, agreements—no one could approach me to steal them. And to kill or harm a vestal was considered a blasphemy that would condemn the perpetrator's soul to the worst pit of hell. Some people think Romans are irreligious, but they're not. They're a very religious people. The documents were safe with me. I was outside the Temple more than most of the girls who served there.

"On the voyage to Atlantis, I often fell in with Atticus. Vestals are not supposed to fraternize with men, and men know this. Atticus respected my status as a pledged woman. But we were together often. On a ship you can't avoid that. Father liked him and invited him to dine with us. When he ate with us, the two of us inevitably got talking. He had read philosophy and knew the Greek poets. Father would doze off from too much wine and too much food. Atticus and I would talk. We enjoyed conversation far into the night while father dozed and snored.

"What can I say? We fell in love. We managed to find time together, especially when we were on the Isle of Atlantis. I was nineteen, he was twenty. We kissed; we planned to run away together. I never coupled with him. The punishment for a vestal who breaks her vow of virginity is to be buried alive. Needless to say, I did not want that. He would face exile and I would face death if anyone even knew we had kissed. So we deiced to call it off. I remember the last time I kissed him. We stood on the deck of that ship under the moonlight and stars, as star appear only above the ocean, blazed in the sky. It broke my heart. I've never stopped loving him through all these years."

My mind came back to the present moment. Claudius waited for Rowena to respond. The pain, tension, and longing showed on her face and in the lines of her body.

"Leave us for a time. We must confer. Tell Atticus I will meet him by the shore when the sun touches the tops of the trees." She stopped and then added, "I will meet him alone." Then she added, "Tell him I am carrying a child. I want him to know that before we confer."

She had not told me she was pregnant, but it did not surprise me.

Claudius nodded. The meeting ended. Gavin and Rowena authorized Claudius and his force to establish camp on the shore by the ship. They pitched tents, set up cooking equipment, lit fires, and began preparing a meal. The whole village by now had come out to gawk at them. Gavin set a guard to keep them at a distance. Still, they could see and were amazed at the large ship, the gleaming gear, and the red uniforms the Romans wore. Some native Britons who had enlisted as Roman auxiliary troops were talking with Gavin's men. The atmosphere did not seem tense. It appeared my newly found people could get along with Romans.

Gavin, Rowena, and I retired to a small room in the Temple to discuss the matter.

I thought Gavin would be against the

proposal. To my surprise, he thought it would work well. His brother lived in a Roman town, he said, where the population of the city was evenly split between colonists and native Britons. The Romans had been in Briton hundreds of years, he pointed out. Whole generations of Romans had been born here and were, a sense, Britons themselves. His brother and their family had prospered in their city. The Romans treated them well. The Roman presence had brought an end to the vendettas, raids, and tribal wars that in the past had made life region so unstable. He said he could endorse the plan if Rowena willed to marry the man.

Still shaken by the turn of events, she replied that she stood as Freya's servant and that even as a married woman she could continue in the rule of priestess. This, she said, would strengthen their position assure people that the Romans would not violate the treaty.

"You are with child," Gavin said. "I did not know this."

"The child's father is Aschel. I became pregnant during one of the times we coupled to release the fullness of Freya's power. As the child is his, it shall be delivered to him when he is born."

"Will Atticus object to this?" I asked, my voice more thick with emotion than I had thought it would be.

"I believe it will make no difference to him." She sat straight and rigid and drew in a long breath. "He is progressive," she said, letting the breath out

It was agreed.

I went home to Brenna. She plied with me with questions about the Romans and what would happen. I had to conceal my grief. Brenna, whom I had once called a child, was a perceptive, intelligent, shrewd woman. I wondered if she were aware of Rowena's and my continuing relationship. Probably, I thought—though if she were she would attribute it to Freya's activity in our lives. I felt weary. My weariness told me I needed to settle into the life the Fates had carved for me here. Atlantis had perished beneath the waves. My wife and children were dead. My friends and family was gone as well. The sea had destroyed my world. I had hoped to reconstruct it with Rowena. She was more like an Atlantian woman and more like Janisa. I saw how I undervalued Brenna. I also knew her well enough to realize she would sense this. An obedient girl who accepted what life had given her, she would not be angry with me—though deep down she would be hurt. I needed to love her without reserve or condescension. She had accepted her life as a captive and slave. Fate had delivered her and blessed her with a husband. Now it was my turn to bow the knee and accept what the Fates had given me and be a blessing to her. They had given me her to me to assuage the pain of loss. My selfishness had led me to disvalue her—a thing that brought shame to my heart when I thought on it. Goodness demanded that I appreciate the gift. Brenna had blessed me with love.

Could any blessing be greater than love?

Things took their course quickly. Rowena met with Atticus, who still loved her and wanted to marry her. He said he did not care she had been intimate with another man. Her pregnancy did not bother him. He agreed to give the child up and said he would hold no animosity toward me as the father. The counsel of the elders approved the match and the treaty. As soon as Rowena bore the child, she would marry Atticus.

As summer turned to fall, the Romans laid the foundation of their colony city, five miles from here. It rose with a speed that astonished everyone. True to Claudius' word, the village prospered. The crews building the city and the road leading to it and soldiers protecting the place bought fish, produce, and grain from us. Some our men hired on as guards and laborers. Relations between our villages and the Romans were cordial.

Brenna bore our second child, a girl, in the winter. I named her Lark, after my oldest daughter. I never apologized to Brenna for how I had disvalued her. Yet I could tell she understood my remorse and accepted my repentance. She understood with her heart and with the silences that a man woman share. The shadow of the past, I resolved, would never come between us, ever again.

Winter was mild. The bay did not freeze. Rowena had our child near the festival of Yule.

A boy. She allowed Brenna and me to name him. We called him Weylen, after Brenna's father, who had been killed in the raid in which she was captured and made a slave. When spring came, Rowena married Atticus.

The night before the wedding, I received a summons to the Temple.

I debated going. Surely she did not want to sleep with me one last time. I asked Brenna what I should do. "She is the priestess of the goddess," she replied. "You must obey her. The goddess has blessed us with children and has provided us with food and warmth—and with safety. You dare not offend her. Go." She kissed me. "I will await your return."

When I came to the Temple, Jannet ushered me into the meeting room. Rowena was there. Kalea stood in attendance on her. Rowena nodded. Kalea got out two glasses and a phial. It took me a moment to recognize it as the last possession I had from my old world. It was the container of Atlantian wine I had on the boat but never got a chance to drink.

"I thought it would be a fitting thing to do. This will bring closure to both our pasts. Our lives were broken and disrupted. I like to think things have come full circle and we can both begin to live again."

I nodded. We drank. The sweetness of the

wine suffused my body. I would never taste anything so delightful again. There would be no more Atlantian wine, just the same as there would be no intimacy with the woman who drank it with me. After we drained our cups, Kalea handed me the phial. It was white, carved from alabaster, the work of a craftsman from the world I had lost.

"Keep this."

"I will."

"I'll miss you, Aschel. What we shared can never die. We will remember it in our hearts as long as we live."

I nodded again. She smiled, breaking her solemnity.

"Of course, it's not like we will never see each other again. We will simply never be lovers. We can begin living new lives—the ones the goddess has given us."

I agreed. Things had gone this way. I remarked that we would have a joyful future.

Brenna and I attended the wedding, which was not as great an affair as I had thought. After Atticus and Rowena were married, they settled down in the newly built city. The colonists farmed the land around the city and began to mine tin, expanding the existing mines and digging new ones. The civil administration built a road and aqueducts. They ended tribal war and revenge killings. Our village continued to sell fish and produce to them. Prosperity came along with the security the presence of the Roman garrison gave.

Rowena continued as priestess of Freya in a temple in the Roman town. Olena and Jannet eventually finished their training and served as priestesses of the temple in our village. Both married. Olena eventually left the service of the temple. Jannet continued as the chief priestess. True to Rowena's word, Kalea left the service of the goddess after three years. The village council returned her children to her. She remarried and, despite her age, had two more healthy sons.

Brenna became pregnant again and bore another girl. Naturally, I named it Trella. Balder continues to grow. He is a strong, bright, beautiful young boy.

The pain of loss comes on me at times. Few people lose a world. Yet the Fates replaced the world I lost with another world, and I thank them for this. I will never again see my wife and children, my father, mother, and brothers. I will never again hear the language I spoke as a child. Yet I have life and I have love. In the end, we can endure most anything if have these, the things most basic, primal, and most true.

David W. Landrum has been published widely in journals and anthologies in the US, UK, Canada, Europe, and Asia. His novellas, *Strange Brew*, *ShadowCity*, *Mother Hulda*, *The Prophetess*, *Le Cafe de la Mort*, and *The Last Minstrel*, are available through Amazon.

THE CRY OF THE LONE COYOTE

The Last Coyote at Little River

Inspired by True Events

Debra Barton

ISBN: 0692799206
ISBN 13: 9780692799208
Library of Congress Control Number: 2016917782
Debra, Manteca, CA